SOUTH PACIFIC

Also by Bill Manhire from Carcanet

Milky Way Bar
(Poetry Book Society Recommendation)

BILL MANHIRE

South Pacific

CARCANET

This selection first published in 1994 by
Carcanet Press Limited
208-212 Corn Exchange Buildings
Manchester M4 3BQ

Grateful acknowledgement is made to the editors of the
following publications in which some of these stories
first appeared: *Chelsea, Edge, Islands, London Magazine,
Meanjin, Metro, PN Review, Span, Sport, Untold*.
'The Brain of Katherine Mansfield' was originally
published as a small book, in Gregory O'Brien's design,
by Auckland University Press.

A CIP catalogue record for this book
is available from the British Library.
ISBN 1 85754 046 8

The publishers acknowledges financial assistance
from the Arts Council of Great Britain

Set in 10pt Concorde by Bryan Williamson, Frome
Printed and bound in England by SRP Ltd, Exeter

Arts Council Funded

For bonny Maisie Aitken

Contents

Cannibals

PART THE FIRST

We were sailing in the Pacific. Seeking out new lands: savages and treasure, sex and mineral rights, you know the sort of thing. Our weaponry very much superior to anything we might meet, the insurance company happy, the holds well stocked, all hands on deck, charts spread out on our knees, tang of sea in our nostrils.

Day after day. Uncle James reading aloud from the Bible.

The South Seas are sprinkled with numberless islands, like stars in the Milky Way. There are whole necklaces of islands, and each jewel on the chain is another paradise.

If the charts are hard to read, that is because of the wild, uncharted waters we are venturing into.

'I love you,' says the ship to the sea. 'We have always been friends, we two, and ever shall be.'

'Yes,' says the sea. 'But oftentimes, when the wind blows high and fierce, I have been greatly troubled for your safety.'

'Yes, dear sea, it is the wind, ever, ever the wind that is making dispeace between us, because it is so seldom in the same mind.'

'True, that is the worst of the wind.'

'How beautifully blue you are today, oh sea, and what tiny wavelets you wear. I never care to go back to the noisy grimy docks when I think of you as you are now.'

'And how beautiful *you* are also, oh ship. Do you know that at a distance you might be mistaken for some bright-winged sea-bird skimming along in the sunshine. But who are these on your deck, oh ship, who make such clamour?'

'They are rough diamonds — sailors, explorers, missionaries. One or two stowaways. The occasional mutineer.'

'Oh well,' says the sea, 'nothing new there, very much the usual stuff.'

You see a peak in the distance, feathery palms and so forth, and you have to admit it's a pretty good feeling.

Our ship slices through the water, breasts the wave, on it goes through the opening in the reef, the *Tia Maria* is its name, I expect I forgot to say that earlier. I am writing on my knees, which is always difficult.

Maps all over the deck. Cap'n Tooth at the helm, old seadog. Excitement mounting. We sail in silver waters beside golden sands.

This island is probably uninhabited, so we will be able to give it a name, that's always a pleasurable thing. Maybe something from the list of names that Gerald keeps in his pocket.

Yes, the island certainly looks uninhabited. Nothing stirring. Any minute now we will lower the rowing boat and men will row ashore for coconuts and just generally try to see what they can see. The rest of us might swim a bit, or maybe sketch the extinct volcano.

'We haven't used Llandudno Junction yet,' says Gerald.

General derision.

Gerald blushes, I'll say that for him, but on he goes, he is totally undeterred.

'Let's see,' he says. 'How about Seattle? Pontypridd? Crofts of Dipple?'

But hold, who are these sinister black creatures who suddenly appear upon the shore, rank upon rank of them, three abreast, uttering cries that chill the very blood in our veins? They skip and howl, they wade into the surf and shake their fists above their heads...

Wait a minute...those black cassocks...those cadaverous smiles...

The priests of Rome! Here before us!

Break out more sail! Away! Away! While yet there is breath in our bodies!

Well, that was a near thing. Touch and go there for a while. Cap'n Tooth breaks out the rum, we decide to call the island Adventure Island, because of the adventure we had there.

'And to think it was so nearly Misadventure Island!' jokes Uncle James.

Gerald scowls below deck, murderous black sharks cruise about our little ship, but our spirits are high.

Tonight I discovered a stowaway in my cabin. It happened thus. I had knelt to say my evening prayers, when my right knee encountered something strange beneath the bunk. Upon investigation, I found a boy secreted there, a sprightly lad clad in denim, who made a dash for the door, one of those absolutely futile things for I caught him easily, even I was surprised at the ease of it, and I threw him forthwith to the floor. Upon which I had my second surprise of the evening.

The young fellow's shirt had torn a little in the course of our struggle, and as I gazed down, panting and victorious, what did I see, peeping out at me, but two quite perfect female breasts...

Well! My stowaway is a girl!

Her name is foreign, it sounds like Meefanwee.

I make frequent overtures of friendship to Meefanwee, and gradually I believe I gain her confidence.

Meefanwee has black hair and green eyes, a really interesting combination.

I shall keep her, I shall be her protector, I shall certainly not let on to Uncle James.

The *Tia Maria* courses on through the vast Pacific. A few days ago we had the adventure with the pirates, that was at Pirate

Island. And just after that there was the island where we couldn't find a place to land. It looked so beautiful and mysterious, just rising up out of the blue Pacific, but we sailed round and round it and failed to find an opening in the coral reef. The crew got tired of our circular motions and fell to muttering among themselves, and Cap'n Tooth had to give them more rum. But at last we were able to sail on and we decided to call the island Mystery Island, because it would always remain a mystery to us.

I keep Meefanwee concealed in my cabin.

She is my little stowaway, that is what I sometimes call her, she looks up into my face trustfully.

Sweet Jesus, it is a look which brings out all the manliness of my soul!

I read to her from the Bible, I touch her private parts.

We have let Gerald name some islands. There were actually three islands together, a group of them, and it was just after the fight with the giant octopus, and of course we were feeling good about that, and we just sort of gave him carte blanche, a French phrase, it means literally white map, I don't think that had ever occurred to me before. I am afraid Gerald rather took advantage of us, and he named the islands after three former girlfriends of his, Yvonne, Sharon and Mrs Llewellyn Davies. The islands were all uninhabited, which Gerald says just make the names even more appropriate.

Actually there were one or two natives, several of us noticed them, but they ran off when they saw us coming.

We dumped the nuclear waste on one of the islands – Sharon, I think, but I don't really remember.

Uncle James has a rather bad snakebite, which he got when he went ashore a few days ago on Mrs Llewellyn Davies. Mrs Appleby, my aunt, is fearfully worried. His leg has swollen to several times its normal size. He cannot enter his cabin, and must lie out on the deck until the swelling subsides. It is a real nuisance:

crew members are always tripping over him and he is constantly having to apologise.

Today there was a message in a bottle, that sometimes happens, I didn't see it myself but someone says there was one. I helped fight off the sandalwood traders, though, that was easy enough, we just opened fire with the really big guns and let them have it. Then we found some pearls, big ones, worth millions apparently, though I personally didn't do any of the diving. But I suppose the real news is the mutiny. I should probably have mentioned it a bit earlier. The crew, led by their own obscure desires, have slain good old Cap'n Tooth and set course for Valparaiso. But not before first putting us ashore on a nearby island.

Uncle James says that we must call our island Fortunate Island — 'for surely good fortune awaits us in this Pacific paradise.'

The island has a lagoon, a coral reef, coconut palms and a mysterious mountain which could be honeycombed with underground passages, it is hard to tell. The island is probably deserted, but we will have to do some proper exploring in the next few days and find a place for signalling ships from and so on.

Meefanwee is safely ashore. I am passing her off as a member of the crew.

'Uncle James,' I say, 'meet Douglas. Douglas, this is my uncle, James Appleby. Douglas was the only one of that riff-raff, mulatto crew, Uncle, with spirit enough to stand by us.'

'Pleased to meet you, my boy,' says Uncle James. 'Sorry I can't get up. My leg is still playing me up a little.'

In fact, Uncle's left leg is now twice the circumference of his upper body, and very, very pustular.

'What a lovely spot this is!'

Uncle James has summoned us all together for words of encouragement. We cluster about him on the sand. He lies like a beached whale.

'Mark these coconut palms, they have borne their fruit year after year, have died, and others have sprung up in their stead;

and here has this spot remained, perhaps for centuries, all ready for man to live in and enjoy.'

He pauses. You can hear the deep incessant boom of distant combers.

'Pray tell, Mr Appleby,' says my aunt, 'what are the great merits of the coconut tree?'

'Why, I'll tell you, madam: in the first place, you have the wood to build a house with; then you have the bark with which you can make ropes and lines, and fishing-nets if you please; then you have the leaves for thatching your house, and also for thatching your head if you please, ho ho, for you may make good hats out of them, and baskets also; then you have the fruit which, as a nut, is good to eat, and very useful in cooking; and in the young nut is the milk, which is also very wholesome; then you have the oil to burn and the shell to make cups of, if you haven't any; and then you can draw toddy from the tree, which is very pleasant when fresh, but will make you tipsy if it is kept too long, ho ho; and then, after that, you may turn the toddy into arrack, which is a very strong spirit. Now there is no tree which yields so many useful things to man, for it supplies him with almost everything.'

'I had no idea of that,' replies the astonished woman. And she goes off to the far end of the beach to peruse her Bible.

'The island is evidently of volcanic origin,' remarks Gerald. 'What is your opinion, William?'

Gerald is addressing me. He and Douglas and I have gone exploring. The others are building a house back at Castaway Bay.

'But remember the reef is coral,' I say. 'Though I suppose the one does not necessarily preclude the other.'

Gerald and I do not really hit it off, I expect that's obvious. I find much of his behaviour unsatisfactory. Welsh, I suppose.

We go along in single file. Hacking through the undergrowth.

Suddenly Douglas screams.

'Oh don't be a girl!' cries Gerald scornfully. 'It's only some old bones.'

'You must think what you will, Gerald,' I quickly interpose. 'But unless I am very much mistaken, those are the rib bones of a man. And those ashes which you poke so idly with a stick, they are signs of cooking. It's as I secretly feared but didn't like to say: before long we shall have cannibals to contend with.'

Douglas snuggles against me.

Gerald stands off to one side and regards us oddly.

I have tried to tell Uncle James of my suspicions. He was sitting on a headland, gazing out to sea. I waved the rib-bone before him. He looked for a moment, but then resumed his inspection of the far horizon.

'Who would ever have imagined, William,' said my uncle, 'that this island, and so many more which abound in the broad Pacific, could have been raised by the work of little insects no bigger than a pin's head.'

'Insects, Uncle?' I replied. 'Oh come now.'

Plop! A coconut fell from a tree.

'Yes, insects. Give me that piece of coral with which you are toying.'

I passed him the rib-bone.

'Do you see, William,' said my uncle after a moment, 'that on every surface there are a hundred little holes? Well in every one of these little holes once lived a sea-insect; and as these insects increase, so do the branches of the coral trees.'

'But an island, Uncle?' I said.

Plop!

'The coral grows at first at the bottom of the sea,' said my uncle wearily. 'There it is not disturbed by wind or wave. By degrees it increases, advancing higher and higher towards the surface; then it is like those reefs you see out there beyond the lagoon, William. Of course it never grows above the surface of the water for if it did the tiny animals would die.'

'Then how does it become an island?'

'By very slow degrees,' said my uncle. 'And frequently the droppings of seabirds play a not inconsiderable part. But run along now William and read your Bible. My leg pains me. I promise we shall speak of this another time.'

Alas, it was not to be. Our time together on Fortunate Island had drawn nearly to an end. Indeed, Uncle James was the first of our number to be captured and eaten by cannibals.

A few days after the conversation I have just set down, Gerald, Douglas and I were out exploring. Gerald walking ahead. Douglas and I secretly holding hands.

We came down to a beautiful sandy bay. Something big, a tree stump or barrel, was rolling in the gentle surf. We ran towards it.

Sweet Jesus! It was the hideously distended leg of my uncle, James Appleby.

I realised at once that my uncle had been captured by cannibals, that these same cannibals had cooked and no doubt eaten him, yet had first removed his swollen limb as a precaution against food poisoning.

We were clearly dealing with a highly intelligent, if savage, people.

It was time to take command.

'Douglas,' I said, 'you are cool; while Gerald, you are fearless. But I am cool *and* fearless, a combination of the qualities you possess individually, and therefore I propose to be your leader, offering cool but fearless leadership. Now let us go at once and warn the others.'

Then rough hands seized me and I knew that the savages had crept up on us even as we talked.

PART THE SECOND

We have been prisoners of the cannibals for several days now. Few of us survived the initial attack; and those among us who have had the fortune (or misfortune!) to keep our lives must witness the savages swaggering past our palisaded compound, patting their bellies and saying the name 'James Appleby' in tones of gratitude and wonder. Our captors seem to be making a special point of fattening the three Appleby girls. The unfortunate young women grow visibly from day to day, probably the steady diet of breadfruit is responsible, and they anxiously inspect their figures in the dress-length mirror which Mange Tout has installed inside the compound.

The leader of the cannibal band is a big, rough man, who names himself Jules Verne, while his lieutenant, the aforementioned Mange Tout, is even more terrible to behold. Mange Tout claims to be the offspring of a shark and a witch, and when he smiles, the row of sharp, triangular teeth which glint along his jaw lends a terrible credence to his tale.

All the same, there is something likeable about the fellow.

I am resolved to find some way of teaching these people Christian precepts. The thing will be to win their confidence. Already a few of them gather each morning for my Bible readings, it's quite encouraging. But each night the drums begin to beat and then the terrible fires glow in the distance. The air fills with the aroma of roasting flesh.

I am deeply puzzled by the cannibals' walk. Often when a group go about together, with Jules Verne at their head, I observe that they will pause. Jules Verne will move his head from side to side and sniff the air; then he will lift his knee up almost to the chin, stepping forward in the same movement, and walk on as before. His men follow in single file, one by one making the same curious motion. It is as if they are stepping over some unseen barrier.

Each night the air fills with songs which chill the blood.

Strip ze skin! Quarter ze body!
Skin, head, hands, feet and bowels —
Set zem aside, oh set zem aside.
We catch ze blood in a pannikin.
We eat ze 'eart and liver first.
Aha! Ho ho! Zut alors!

We clutch one another for comfort. Douglas and I do, anyway. So do Gerald and poor Mrs Appleby. Also the two remaining

Appleby girls. The eldest girl, Madge, has already been carried off to the cannibal kitchen.

Each day I am taken to visit Jules Verne in his headquarters, we talk together, we chew the fat. It is probably the fact that I have given him a jigsaw of Edinburgh Castle that makes him favour me in this way. Usually I help him find the four corners; then he sets to and makes it up during the day, destroying it again at nightfall.

Another thing that has happened is I have taught Jules and his closest advisers how to play Monopoly. They seem to have an instinctive understanding of the game. I may have forgotten to say that with all the confusion during the mutiny I managed to smuggle away a few things like that, things that would be good for trading. They have certainly come in handy.

We all make sure Jules wins, of course. By the end of a typical game, Jules owns most of London, while I have spent many rounds languishing in jail!

Strange to say, I believe I am beginning to win the respect of these rough, untutored South Sea Islanders. Gerald, always quick to offer an opinion, says that they are not South Sea Islanders at all, but French adventurers who have stayed in the Pacific so many years that they have descended to a savage condition. But this seems highly implausible.

The cannibals are certainly not Christians. They worship a mysterious creature whom they address by the name 'Zodiac'. After their evening feasting, they gather on the shores of the lagoon, a terrifying sight in the moonlight, and cry the name of their god. They make strange huffing and puffing noises, and their strange stepping motions.

Of course there is debate amongst our little party, but I am of the view that the cannibals are not entirely devoid of intelligence.

I dream of the day when these frank, unlettered creatures will bring me their idols and cry: 'Take zese zings, zese *Zodiacs*. Zey were once our gods, but now we are ashamed of zem. Take zem 'ence, for we wish zat we never more may behold zem again!'

But each night the cannibal drums beat out their messages of death. The second Appleby girl, her name slips my mind, has been taken away. And Mange Tout, when he came yesterday to clean the mirror, stared at Mrs Appleby for several minutes and said something about the annual widow-strangling ceremony.

I have taken to spying on Gerald and my aunt. Gerald is a regular rascal where a pretty girl is concerned.

They spend hours and hours together in the far corner of the compound. They believe they are unobserved.

Gerald lies on his back, and Mrs Appleby smoothes back the curly chestnut hair from his temples.

'Would you like to have me for a mama?' she asks.

'I would rather have you — for — for —'

Gerald hesitates.

'Well, dear, for what? Speak out,' says Mrs Appleby in an encouraging tone.

'I was going to say, for a sweetheart, ma'am. You are so very lovely.'

'Am I lovely?' my aunt repeats, looking at her handsome figure in the looking glass. Running the palms of her hands across her hips.

The hot blood mounts to Gerald's face and makes it burn.

'How you blush! Why do you blush so?' she says.

'I don't know, ma'am. It comes to me when I talk to you, I think. I have these stirrings in my loins.'

'Strings in your loins?' exclaims my aunt. 'Why, how very strange! But you cannot have me for a sweetheart, Gerald. I am a widow in mourning, and the aunt of your young friend, William. At all events, we shall soon be eaten by these cannibals.'

'Still, I may love you quietly and at a distance, ma'am. You cannot help people loving you.'

'You funny boy,' she exclaims. 'Come here, you funny boy.'

And soon, I am afraid, she is all over him.

I have solved the problem of the cannibals' walk. Jules Verne believes that there are deadly invisible rays stretched across the surface of the island, they are like wires drawn taut a few inches above the ground. When Jules pauses and sniffs, lifting his knee towards his chin, he is first locating, then stepping over, these treacherous obstacles.

I have all this from Mange Tout, who has begun to confide in me and is plainly sceptical of the mysterious rays. Yet he, and the rest of Jules Verne's savage band, follow their leader in every point. Occasionally one of them will trip, or pretend to trip, then fall to the ground howling. At such moments, Jules Verne laughs hideously; and all those still on their feet join in.

The cannibals take very great care in the preparation of their food. Perhaps Gerald is right after all, there is certainly a Gallic quality to that. They took away the last of the Appleby girls this morning, and Mange Tout tells me in confidence that, after she has been bled, she will be marinaded for several hours before the actual process of cooking commences.

They anoint Miranda — that is her name, Miranda — they anoint her with quassia chips and rue, with the root of tormentil and ears of barley, with slippery elm powder and the bark of wild cherry, with bladderwrack and pulp of the banyan, olibanum gum and coltsfoot, with wood betony and extract of underquil.

In the distance, the terrible drums begin again.

Each day when I am escorted to Jules Verne's headquarters to play Monopoly, I find myself pretending to step over the invisible rays. It is surprisingly easy to get into the habit. Jules Verne is most impressed by my behaviour and has explained to me that the rays are most dense around the headquarters building itself. The closer you approach, the greater number of wires.

Near Jules Verne's hut is the impaled head of my uncle James Appleby. He gazes out to sea through sightless eyes, as though he is scanning the horizon for a sail. A sail he knows will never come.

These cannibals do not eat the heads of their victims, they preserve them, and the procedures are really rather elaborate. Mange Tout has begun to instruct me in the treatment of heads.

We are at the Monopoly board.

'If the head is very much larger than the neck,' says Mange Tout, 'you must cut the throat lengthwise to remove the head. It is immaterial whether the eyes are taken out before the head is skinned or after.'

Jules Verne passes Go.

'The gouge,' continues Mange Tout, 'should go well to the back of the eye and separate the ligament which holds it to the socket. Should the gouge go into the eye,' warns Mange Tout, 'it will let out the moisture, which often damages the skin. Some people,' he continues, 'crush the skull slightly to make it come out of the skin easily, but this I do not personally advise.'

Jules Verne puts a hotel on Mayfair.

'Remove the brains,' says Mange Tout, 'by taking out a piece of skull at the back as you cut off the neck. This we did in the case of your late uncle, James Appleby, and it really worked rather well. Then you must pull the eyes out of their cavity and fill up their place with wool soaked in arsenical soap. Anoint the head and neck well with arsenical soap, and place in the neck a piece of stick covered with wool, the end of which you must slip into the hole already made in the skull for extracting the brains.'

Mange Tout breaks off and grins with delight. He smiles with every muscle in his head! He has just won $10.00 in a Beauty Contest. Jules Verne looks somewhat put out, he is not really much of a sport.

But look — there! — how the smile grows fixed on Mange Tout's face, a rictus of despair, a rictus of defeat, and he falls, he falls suddenly across the Monopoly board, scattering all the houses and hotels of central London. A spear is embedded in his back.

The air fills with howls and eldritch screams. Oh crikey! Another band of cannibals is attacking. Jules Verne and his men rush to join battle with the enemy, they are not afraid. But head over heels they go over their own invisible tripwires and are quickly defeated.

Cries of the slaughtered. The greedy earth drinks the blood of the dead.

It is hard to be sure what to make of this new development. Have we been rescued? And if so, who has rescued us? Or have we fallen into the hands of even more ferocious savages?

PART THE THIRD

It has been a time of pain and dark confusion, and I have lost all sense of time. I seem to be alone. Mrs Appleby was here, I think, my brief companion in captivity, but then was taken away. For a time I heard her cries at intervals. Then, after a time, nothing.

Time passes.

There has been no sign of Douglas/Meefanwee or of Gerald, perhaps they escaped, who knows, perhaps they were killed during the fighting between the rival bands of cannibals, it is as if they never existed. For the moment I must assume that they are dead — as dead as Jules Verne and his unfortunate followers.

I pass in and out of consciousness. Sometimes I think I can hear Meefanwee's voice, its ringing, bell-like laughter. Oh, it is like the sound of water running over stones! Then I ache for all that was mine and now is mine no longer, I ruefully touch my bruises. Then I begin to believe I can hear the raucous laughter of Gerald. He sounds as if he is drunk, laughing at his own jokes.

I fear I am delirious.

The other thing is that I seem to be underground — there are damp rock walls. What meagre light there is, comes from flaming torches. Ghastly shadows flicker across the walls and roof. My guess is that I am deep in the heart of the extinct volcano.

But hark! Rough voices, footsteps, cursings in a foreign tongue. The door of my cavern rasps open...

I am being alternately pushed and dragged, I hardly know which, through a series of dark, winding passages. On and on, I do not think I can endure much more, but then I am thrust out into a vast underground chamber. At the far end of this immense cavern are a hundred cannibal warriors, all in their battle finery, prostrate before a raised throne on which sits... a woman. The sight fills me with terror.

Dark of hair, dark of eye. Shoulderless dress and elaborate tattoos. But surely her features are those of a European? How strange.

And who is that who sits at her right hand, laughing and grunting, the torchlight flickering cruelly across his face? The hateful Gerald! There he sits beside the savage queen. As cool as a cucumber. Like some denizen of Hell.

'Gerald!' I cry. 'Where is Mrs Appleby?'

Gerald looks shifty.

I feel the woman's eyes on me, her gaze travels up and down my body, it is almost immodest, a woman her age, she must be nearly fifty.

'Well, my young friend, you present me with an interesting problem. Shall I let you go, or shall you be my victim? Ha! Ha! Ha!'

She breaks into peals of hideous laughter.

'For pity's sake, your Highness!' I fall to my knees.

Gerald chuckles. Pleasure fairly swaggers across his features.

'William,' he says, 'may I introduce you to Mrs Llewellyn Davies.'

PART THE FOURTH

Well, how extraordinary!

We have been talking excitedly all evening. I have not been a prisoner at all, just sick with a sudden fever, probably from drinking the cannibal wine.

How strangely things have turned out! It seems that Mrs Llewellyn Davies is Gerald's old landlady. Gerald named an island after her earlier in the story. Well, she was more than his landlady, I suppose that's obvious. She ran a rooming house in Bangor, and Gerald lived there when he was doing his teacher training.

Meefanwee is not Meefanwee. I had the spelling wrong, she is Myfanwy. She is actually Mrs Llewellyn Davies' daughter. It is not clear who her father was, but it seems that Gerald is an obvious candidate, at any rate Myfanwy calls him 'Father'. Apparently when Myfanwy was a child her mother vanished, but the lonely child never believed the story about her mother being dead, and after she left high school she began to search the broad Pacific, she never gave up hope. She had adventure after adventure, of course, the Pacific is that sort of place, and one day she disguised herself as a boy, stowed away on a ship called the *Tia Maria* and, well, the rest is history...

The only wrong note in all this is Mrs Appleby. I am afraid that Mrs Llewellyn Davies found out about her relationship with Gerald and at once gave her to her savage followers. They feasted on her flesh that evening. Gerald does not seem to mind.

'But how ever did Mrs Llewellyn Davies — sorry, your mother — come to be here in the first place? Queen of a cannibal island and everything?'

I am talking to Myfanwy. We are down at the beach, we have been swimming in the clear lagoon, there is one of those astonishing sunsets out beyond the reef.

'Put your hand there, William, yes there, that's it, mmm that's lovely.'

'Well?'

'Well what, William?'

'Well are you going to answer my inquiry about your mother?'

'Oh *that*! Well, William, I have not quite gathered all of the details yet, I am just so happy to have found her at last. But you will remember that years ago a Welsh rugby supporters' tour group went missing, it was after the tour itself had finished — traditional forward dominance had told against us, as everyone predicted — and they went on a Pacific Island cruise, the supporters I mean, not the team, it was part of the original package.'

I nod.

'Well, William, as you probably also know, the boat disappeared, just vanished off the face of the earth, it was in all the newspapers at the time, no one could make any sense of it. Oooh, that's so good, press a little harder, oh yes darling. Well, it seems that the cruise ship was rammed by a mysterious submarine — Russian, French, American, no one seems to know. But the ship simply broke apart. It was all over in a matter of minutes. Everyone went to the bottom.'

'Except your mother,' I interpose.

'Except my mother. You see, she had been playing deck rugby, and was fortunate enough to be holding the ball at the precise moment of collision. Mother clung to the ball for dear life, it kept her afloat, she simply clung to it, hardly knowing what she was doing, till eventually she was washed up on the shores of this island, just a few yards from where we presently sit. It saved her life, you know, that rugby ball.'

'What a piece of luck! How extraordinary!'

'Yes, this is one of those cases where the truth is very much stranger than fiction.'

'But how did she come to acquire such power over these savage islanders?' I ask. 'She does not seem to be especially Christian, yet it is truly wonderful, the way in which they are obedient to her. And why did she attack Jules Verne? Had she seen you and Gerald, do you think, and set out to rescue you, or what?'

'I cannot say, William. It may simply be the volatile politics of the South Pacific. But I have not yet pursued these matters with her, so for the moment they must remain loose ends. Surely you can cope with a few loose ends, my darling? Now, would you like me to put my hand somewhere on you, what about there, shall I touch you there, does that feel good?'

I have resolved to build a raft. Myfanwy is helping me, she is sorry to see me bent on departure but she understands when I tell her I cannot have Gerald for a father-in-law, it is simply out of the question. The raft is made from the trunks of that selfsame tree whose merits were expounded, so long ago, by my late uncle, James Appleby. How little we guessed what lay in store! And even Uncle James could not have known that I would one day find a use for the coconut tree which even he had failed to anticipate!

From time to time Myfanwy and I embrace as of old, but now there is a distance. The sadness of departure lies between us.

During the day I work at building my raft. At night we join the others and listen to Mrs Llewellyn Davies read from her Visitors Book, she does a few entries each evening, the whole tribe assembles.

'The weather exceeded only by the company' — Littleford family, Birmingham.
'Vielen Dank!' — Familie G. Prutz, Hamburg.
'Thank you, very nice' — Jim and Noeline Carter, Tasmania.

The cannibals think it is a sacred book. After each entry they gasp and applaud. They show their appreciation in the usual manner.

I look out at the lagoon, at the clouds of spray above the reef, seabirds diving and calling... and beyond lies all the vastness of the blue Pacific!

My raft is ready, it is time to go.

I shall be adrift for days, maybe for weeks. But eventually some ship will spot my ragged sail, heave to and take me aboard, faint and delirious from the pitiless sun, full of a wild story, cannibals and a mutiny, poor fellow, look! is that a Bible he is clutching, take him below...

I gaze on Myfanwy, my companion in so many trials. I take her photograph. I touch her lips, her hair, her perfect breasts. Then I turn to go. That is how it is, adventure and regret, there is no getting away from it, we live in the broad Pacific, meeting and parting shake us, meeting and parting shake us, it is always touch and go.

Some Questions I am Frequently Asked

Q. Through here? Are you sure? Through the wardrobe?

A. Yes, mind your head. It's quite low in there. Just push on through.

Q. Oh, I see, there's a door at the back.

A. Yes, it's like a secret entrance. It's like having to enter a *Boy's Own* adventure story before you can sit down and start writing.

Q. And you actually write through here?

A. Yes. It's private, obviously: no one bothers me. But it's also a good spot in summer, lots of sun and the big blue curtains. And then in winter it can be quite cosy. The starbelly stove makes a big difference.

Q. Do you follow a strict routine, then? Do you come through here every morning?

A. Well, I'm usually at my desk by nine each day. I write in a painstaking longhand, in exercise books bought for me by my son Pablo expressly for the purpose. I work through to about one o'clock, all things being equal, and by then Mrs Austen has prepared me a light meal of green peppers and sasquebette.

Q. Is part of that time spent revising? Do you revise much?

A. Oh, revision is certainly important. After I have eaten a light lunch of peppers and sasquebette, Mrs Austen clears away.

We chat for a while perhaps, and then usually I stroll along the clifftops, Punch comes with me, and I might stare out at the islands. Phrases occur to me, they always do, and I try to remember them. I have a superstitious feeling that I must not write these phrases down at the moment they come to me, that they are not given for this purpose. Perhaps this is something that will interest your readers? Then in the evening, if the thought appeals, I make my way across the paddocks to the local hotel. Some of the regulars are real characters. Occasionally I take notes.

Q. I've read somewhere that there are quite large sasquebette plantations on some of the islands. Have you written about them? The islands, I mean?

A. Not yet, but I would like to.

Q. Have you written about the hotel? I can't recall anything. Actually, let me just play that back. It would be terrible if the batteries were flat or something, just the sort of thing that happens to me.

A. Not yet, but I would like to.

Q. Sorry about that, I just had this feeling all of a sudden that I'd better check. I see several yellow exercise books on the table over there. Does that mean you're working on something at the moment?

A. Yes. A novel.

Q. Can you say something about it?

A. I don't think I wish to talk about it, because that might be to take the whole enterprise for granted. One of the great rules in this business is, never discuss work in progress.

Q. Oh well…

A. But I can read you a little. Here is how it starts:

> The coup leader calls around. There is a small evening breeze, it shakes the bamboo at the bottom of the garden.

Birds cling there — at the centre of the grove, hidden from view, they sleep and sway.

It is hard to go on thinking of him as Malcolm. It is strange how the uniform makes a difference.

He has brought me a Dennis Wheatley novel: *The Devil Rides Out*. It sits on the table between us.

'What would it be?' he says. 'Twenty years?'

The book has my name in it. The handwriting is mine. Malcolm says he borrowed it when we were both at school together.

We sit on the verandah and watch the stars above the bamboo, the southern constellations. We talk about Monsoon Asia with Bully Ferguson, the coloured chalk maps he made on the blackboard. Classmates. Far-off days. Have I seen anything of Gary and Jim? Do I know how they are doing? Tom is in Hamilton, still pulling teeth, have we kept in touch? And so on and so on and so on. Then —

'We need you, Philip.'

My fame as newsreader. As a media personality.

'If it would make things easier, think of it as a personal favour — old times sort of thing.'

My skills with the autocue. My knowledge of current affairs. My reassuring manner. My air of quiet authority. My Liberty tie.

'You have a way of reading the news,' says Malcolm, 'I don't know how you do it but you do, so that every single viewer feels *included*. Did you know that?

I say nothing. He makes a mark on his clipboard.

He offers me Antarctica, sections of Australia, mistresses with great smooth marbly limbs...

Or am I imagining this?

I agree to think it over. We walk down to the gate together.

The woman next door is out on the footpath, calling the name of her dog. *Fairburn! Fairburn!*

Men stand at attention, they salute Malcolm as he climbs

into the waiting limousine. The stars above. The southern constellations.

Malcolm drives away beneath an evening moon.

That's just short of an A4 page, single spacing. I'm not sure about the present tense, now that I read the thing out loud. It sounds a bit mannered, perhaps. How does it come across to you?

Q. Fine; it's really good.

A. I hope you're not just saying that.

Q. No, I really thought it was excellent. Actually it's the names in there that fascinate me. Why do you use names like Malcolm and Philip?

A. Well, why anything, I suppose. They're just names, it isn't something I've thought about a great deal, I must say…

Q. It's just that they seem so *ordinary*, the names themselves. And I don't think of your *writing* as ordinary. So I thought it must be deliberate.

A. Well, probably not for me to say — though I don't wish to reject your observation out of hand. But Fairburn, for what it's worth, turns out to be the absolutely crucial character in there.

Q. The dog?

A. Yes.

Q. Fascinating. Do you have a dog yourself?

A. I used to have one, but alas I shot it by accident a few months ago — I was firing at an intruder. So that was the end of Michelle. I haven't had the heart to replace her. Still, I winged the intruder, I'm pleased to say.

Q. Right…let me just look at this list of questions here…Ah yes, do you have a favourite work?

A. Of my own?

Q. Yes.

A. I think that *Banks* is probably the most *successful* thing I've done. There was the film and so forth.

Q. That's the novel about Sir Joseph Banks and his ten servants?

A. Yes.

Q. The thing I like about it is the way you have the ten chapters, you know, with each one being from the point of view of one of the ten servants. But Banks himself isn't even *named* in the text, is he?

A. No.

Q. I think it's really clever, the way that works.

A. Well, you're very kind. They turned it into cheap costume drama, the film people: sex and sailing ships. But I can't say that it *interests* me very much any more. The thing I like best is a little poem called 'Murihiku Wagon Music', which *Landfall* rejected, did you know, years ago. Now they beg me to send them things, of course.

Q. Would you like to be Maori?

A. Pardon?

Q. Would you like to be Maori? It's a question I'm asking every writer, well, all the Pakeha writers. The Maori writers, the ones who'll talk to me, I ask them if they'd like to be Pakeha. I get some interesting responses.

A. Well I actually have a little Maori blood…

Q. But how do you *identify?* That's the real issue.

A. On days that are merely overcast, I think of myself as Maori. But when it rains I am Pakeha, soaked to the skin.

Q. That's it? That's what you're going to say?

A. That will have to do. I shall have to disappoint you. I used to be all for the joys of simple sunbathing, of course, back in the days when we still had an ozone layer.

Q. Fair enough. But what's your *location?* As a person. Imaginatively speaking. I know you travel, I know you speak a lot of languages. Do you think of yourself as a specifically New Zealand writer?

A. Ah, that is a question I am frequently asked, and here is my answer, which is a little oblique and takes the form, more or less, of a letter. Someone is being addressed but you will have to imagine this person. This time, no names.

Beloved!

I'm sorry!

I forgot that we were engaged to be married

I forgot that just for a while there

we were seeing something of each other. Yes I got drunk and played around, well of course. Yet just for a while there it was all courtship phase, we were on a ship's deck, singing our way to land, we courted each other word by word, we went up or down the charts, I don't remember. You stood and I stood: we gazed at one another across the sitting and kneeling members of the gamelan orchestra, the farmyard full of dark, metallic birds, a pair of shadow puppets who watched the quality of the light, who waited for the light to fade, mere tourists struggling with the view, and people put their hands together in the usual fashion, there was applause, I remember it well, and that was the very moment that I fell in love.

But what about you?

Q. Me? How do you mean?

A. No, not *you*. Not in this tiny narrative sequence. This is still the letter.

Q. Oh, sorry.

A. I'll continue.

Q. Yes. I'm really sorry.

A. Then, just last week, long after you were gone, long after you were gone, I heard a repeat broadcast of your ten-minute radio talk on the current state of New Zealand English. There was your voice again, it spoke of tag phrases and commas, it discoursed upon its own rising inflections. Did we really speak like that? But you were my beloved, you were supposed to treat me well, where were you? Late at night I listened to the silence in the radio, the noise of rain after the station closes down. Where were you? Then I went to an old friend's funeral, and at the crematorium, cream and gold, afteer a few sad words, they played both sides of *Astral Weeks*. Beloved, oh beloved, those are the sort of people I used to go around with. The living feel rejected by the dead — not so much left behind as pushed away. That is something I have come to think. As for *Astral Weeks*, the truth is that some of it lasts and some of it doesn't.

There we are.

Q. Pardon?

A. That's it. I've finished the letter. The answer to your question.

Q. I have to admit I haven't taken it all in. It's very *rich*. Were you inventing it as you went along, or is it a thing you do by heart?

A. Oh. I extemporise each time. But you can use your machine to play it back later, you'll find it makes some sort of sense.

Q. Well, it's an astonishing view from up here.

A. Yes, on a clear day you can see the outer islands. There's a tree on one of them — Little Tartan or Big Tartan, I don't know which — and people say that if you climb it in the right weather conditions, after twenty-four hours of rain is one of the important elements, I seem to remember, you can see Australia.

Q. Australia. Really?

A. I don't know if you saw a man with a rifle in the gardens as you came up?

Q. Yes. He stared at me...

A. Well that would have been my brother-in-law, Punch. He's a useful fellow. Anyway, it was Punch who planted the tree — about ten years ago. It's just a young South Island rata. But the thing is, it was Punch who started the story, he put it around quite deliberately. And now it has a life of its own. It just goes to show. Of course, people are very gullible.

Q. This is probably a rather obvious question, but did you always want to be a writer?

A. I don't ever remember making a conscious decision. The rainy days came and went. But I don't remember a time when I thought I would be anything else. I wrote the usual little tales and rhymes when I was a child.

Q. Did you have a happy childhood?

A. Oh yes. Certainly as a young child, until I was ten. But then things changed.

Q. Changed? How do you mean?

A. My mother lay seriously ill. She sat up in bed at the transplant hospital, her hands crossed over her breasts. She rocked a little. Weakness, weakness: she needed a new heart. Photographers came and went. There was the public appeal, you see. She gave a wan smile at appropriate moments.

My father drove to the hospital. He had made a list of cheerful things to say. He was a gloomy man in his early forties, hair already grey yet plenty of it, and he rehearsed his list of cheerful things as he turned right into Murihiku Road, not particularly looking to see what was coming. His last words were: 'new vacuum cleaner'.

Q. New vacuum cleaner?

A. Yes, he was planning to buy one. I was in the back seat with my two sisters. None of us were hurt. I think Glenys had bruised ribs, something like that.

Q. Your father died, then…

A. My mother lay waiting at the transplant hospital, wondering if there was some delay. Meanwhile the organ transplant unit took my father's heart to the hospital, they opened my mother's chest, sawing through the bone with a small handsaw which is kept expressly for this purpose. They wedged her ribs open, a breast on each side of her body, and they removed her heart and replaced it with my father's. The operation took six hours, and two days later she was sitting up in bed drinking a cup of tea.

Q. Amazing. I don't think you've written about any of this…

A. She came home for Christmas dinner. The newspapers carried photographs of her in a party hat: Mother opening a box of chocolates, Mother pulling a cracker, Mother smiling broadly. Then she started to slip. They can do a lot more than they used to, but eventually everyone starts to slip. My sisters and I sat at her hospital bedside, intensive care, she was singing her way to shore, her skin was golden, jaundiced, and the bottles above her head filled slowly with yellow phlegm, they were draining her lungs as part of their attempt to manage her condition. It was essentially a management problem. My sisters and I sat and watched her. The look on her face! I have spent my life trying to describe it. She was rejecting my father's heart.

The doctors issued a press release which said she had died of 'uncontrollable rejection'. There was a big funeral service, lots of people from the press and radio and television, and even a representative of the then Minister of Health, who made himself known to us afterwards. Of course, this was in the days when we still had a Minister of Health.

Q. So you were made an orphan at the age of ten. Your sisters, too.

A. Yes. The way I think of it now, we were the victims of uncontrollable rejection. For years after that, I went to my room straight after tea and slammed the door. My aunt thought I was crying, but I was singing. I was listening to the radio, I was learning the songs of uncontrollable rejection. All those sad songs you sing along to, all that obvious music. The golden oldies. The blasts from the past...

Q. Well, I don't know what to ask you next...

A. Come and look at this, then.

Q. I've actually got lots of other questions.

A. But come and look all the same.

Q. The poster on the wall? I was wondering actually, earlier on ...all the diagrams and things.

A. The whole thing is a kind of prophetic chart, it tells the future. It's something Napoleon used to consult, or so they say.

Q. That's why his picture's there! I was wondering.

A. Yes. There's a whole set of questions, you can probably see, and the idea is you ask a question and then work out which answer applies to you. Would you like to try?

Q. Well, yes, if you're sure... It sounds interesting.

A. All right, make five rows of dashes, if you would please, on this sheet of paper — roughly twelve marks to a row, but don't consciously try to count to twelve or anything. All right? Here, use this pencil.

Q. Like this? Is this right?

A. Yes, that's it. Okay, and now I can work out that your code mark looks...like this...and now all you have to do is cast your eye over the questions and choose one you'd like to ask.

Q. This column here?

A. Yes, any of those.

Q. All right. Let's see... Will my name be immortalised, and will posterity applaud it? Shall I ever recover from my present misfortunes? Are absent friends in good health, and what is their present employment? Shall I ever find a treasure?

A. Sorry, I thought I said at the start: you can only have one question.

Q. Oh, I realise that, I'm just deciding. Thinking aloud. All right ... Shall I be successful in my present undertaking?

A. That's your question?

Q. Yes. Shall I be successful in my present undertaking?

A. Hang on then... let's look...

> This is a question I am frequently asked, and here is my answer: 'Examine thyself strictly, oh luckless wight, whether thou oughtest not to abandon thy present intentions. For thou shalt be turned away, and never know it.'

Q. Well!

A. Sometimes it can be a bit discouraging.

Q. What does wight mean?

A. I believe it's an old fashioned way of saying person.

Q. Oh... All right, then. Does the person whom I love, love and regard me?

A. Just one question, remember?

Q. Sorry, I forgot. Well, I'd better ask you a few more questions before the tape runs out.

A. Fine. Off you go.

Q. Do you revise a lot?

A. Not really.

Q. Do you have a favourite piece of work?

A. Always the piece I'm currently working on.

Q. Do you read reviews of your work?

A. Hardly ever.

Q. What happens to Philip?

A. Pardon?

Q. Philip, in your new novel.

A. I wish I could tell you. But I mentioned earlier, I have a policy about work in progress.

Q. Sorry. I was forgetting…

A. Oh, turn that thing off a minute then.

Q. The tape recorder?

A. Yes.

Q. Okay, it's going again. That's fascinating. The Ministry of Rain idea. Do you think Philip *deserves* to have all that happen to him, though?

A. Well, Philip says: 'I'm sorry, Malcolm, I'm going to have to say no.' And Malcolm says: 'You're saying no?' And Philip says: 'Yes, I'm going to have to say no.'

Q. End of Philip.

A. You could say that.

Q. He's certainly a very tedious character.

A. Pardon?

Q. I said, do you get many visitors here?

A. People turn up. I usually turn them away.

Q. Do you believe we are put on this earth for a purpose?

A. Sorry?

Q. Do you believe we are put on this... Look, what are you doing now?

A. Sorry?

Q. What are you doing now? With that thing?

A. I am coming towards you in a threatening manner — the manner I adopt when confronting intruders.

Q. Why? Look... Stay away from me!

A. It's all right, calm down. Just my little joke. That is how I turn away unwanted visitors. It works rather well.

Q. Oh.

A. But you will have gathered that I am tired, we must bring this discussion to an end. My son Pablo will be waiting to see you to the door. Punch will be waiting to see you to the gate. And I expect your editor will be waiting for you to return with all this splendid material you must have.

Q. I'm sorry, I thought you were serious.

A. I wasn't.

Q. No.

A. Well, time to be going back through the wardrobe.

Q. Funny, I can't actually see where it is. Whereabouts did we come in?

A. Do you see that tall black painting, the one on the sheet of corrugated iron?

Q. Over there? Yes. Isn't that a painting by...

A. Yes, that's the one. Well, that painting masks the door through to the wardrobe.

Q. Really! That's ingenious.

A. Punch rigged it up, he's a clever fellow.

Q. One last question. Do you have any tips for aspiring writers?

A. Don't be put off by the first few rejection slips. They're just one of life's little eventualities.

Q. One last question.

A. Yes?

Q. What do you think of these new starbelly stoves? Has yours worked out all right?

A. That is a question I am frequently asked, and here is my answer: They save space, give out a great deal of heat, and are extremely fuel efficient.

Q. That's good to know. I've been thinking of getting one, but it's quite an outlay, and you hear all sorts of conflicting reports.

A. Well, I will say one word to you. Fuel. You have to get the length of the logs exactly right. I like to saw my own. Each autumn I have a truckload of wood dumped down at the bottom of the garden, just behind the bamboo grove.

Q. So you saw the timber up yourself?

A. Indeed. Why, Punch and I were working down there earlier in the day, before you arrived. I was quietly working the handsaw back and forth when suddenly a weta fell to the ground — in two neat pieces. Sad, ugly, damaged creature.

Q. Ugh!

A. I had sawn it in half somehow. The two bits lay there for a moment. Then the head ran furiously from the body, scuttled away under the woodpile. But the body... the body stayed quite still, didn't budge — as if it knew there was absolutely no point in trying to give chase. That made me feel odd... I had to sit down...

Q Uncontrollable rejection!

A. Sorry?

Q. The bit of body that was left behind...

A. Yes?

Q. It was suffering from uncontrollable rejection.

A. Yes...

Q. Your old friend!

A. Yes. Probably. Now, if you think you might need a photograph, ask Mrs Austen on the way out, and she can let you have something from the box.

Q. Thank you. Just one last question.

A. Yes.

Q. Will you sign this for me?

A. This?

Q. Yes.

A. This?

Q. Yes.

A. No.

Ponies

It was just after the assassination of Indira Gandhi that I came into the employ of Jason Michael Stretch. Wellington is a city of hidden steps and narrow passages, dark tributary corridors which are rapidly being translated, courtesy of the new earthquake codings, into glittering malls and arcades, whole worlds of space-age glass and silver. Inside these places, on their several levels, there is a curious calm, which is now beginning to extend out on to the footpaths. No one points excitedly; people drift along, pale, ice-cold, gazing into windows in a way which is almost tranquil, or ride escalators which take them up and down but not quite anywhere. A few years ago — as, say, a first-year student — I think I might well have scorned these aimless citizens, or felt sorry for them: a bit superior, anyway. Now they strike me as somehow beyond distress or temptation or anyone's genuine concern — as if they are busy at something which the city itself expects of them, and which they do rather well merely by moving from one place to the next.

A few people behave as if they know their way around. They lack the general air of glazed serenity. They don't quite merge into the crowd. They move marginally faster, like swimmers going downstream, outpacing the current; then they duck clear and vanish into a doorway or make a sudden dash across the road into the downtown traffic. For a few weeks I was running so many errands for Jason Stretch that I began to fancy that I myself must have looked like this. A man who stood out a little from the crowd. A *busy* fellow, someone with intentions and a destination.

Pepperell and Stretch was in Upper Cuba Street — down an alleyway, up a flight of steps, several turns along a corridor. The footpath in that part of Cuba Street has a richness which not only assaults your nostrils, it manages to hit you right at the back of the throat — as if having soaked up a full variety of human juices over the years it is eager to give something back. (You will see that in my weaker moments I would like to be a writer, not a part-time student of anthropology who has got himself lost somewhere between courses.) But maybe it is only because of the Chinese restaurant on the corner that someone with a spraycan has written Pong Alley just next to Drop the Big One — two messages which I had the opportunity to contemplate several times a day as I went by lugging a bag filled with items for the mail or yellow leaflets for one of Jason's suburban letterbox runs.

There wasn't a Pepperell, not in the office. One of my jobs, though, was to take the Number 1 bus out to Island Bay once a week and remove from the letterbox of a house in Evans Street the about-to-be-current issue of *Pepperell's Investment Weekly*, a stockmarket tip sheet, all immaculately typed and centred on a sheet of white A4 paper. Then the thing would be to take this back to town, over to Easiprint in Taranaki Street, and get fifty-seven copies run off ('Pepperell and Stretch's charge account thanks'); and that same day if there was time, or the next morning if there wasn't, I'd trundle back out to Evans Street, ring the doorbell, go and stare at the island for half an hour — and back again to find each of the fifty-seven sheets signed, 'All the best! Bob Pepperell', in a ragged blue ballpoint.

Mrs Watson said that the woman before her had told her that Jason had acquired *Pepperell's Investment Weekly* when he took over the firm, and that he had actually been a subscriber himself when he was still in Balclutha. Mrs Watson typed subscriber addresses on envelopes for me to slide the individually signed sheets into. She did one or two other jobs of the same sort; otherwise she typed student theses, paying Jason Stretch a 20 per cent commission fee. She said this figure was 'very fair'. Jason looked after the horoscopes himself.

'A terrible business, this shooting in India,' said Jason Stretch. 'Two of Mrs Gandhi's bodyguards shot her seven times as she was walking from her home to an interview with the British actor Peter Ustinov. One of the assassins had been one of Mrs Gandhi's bodyguards for eight years. The entire security unit of Mrs Gandhi's residence has been taken off duty and is undergoing intensive questioning. Unquote.'

He put down the *Dominion* and reached across the desk. I reached out my hand, since this was what he seemed to be expecting, and he took it. He shook it. (Was the grasp firm or limp?) 'Executed in cold blood by her own employees,' he said. 'These all have to be read for clipping and filing.' He gestured towards a pile of newspapers. 'Still, I doubt if you'll have time for that sort of thing. I very much hope you won't. Well, there we are. Nine o'clock tomorrow, then. Let's see how things go, Kevin.'

Well, there we were. As they say. I am inventing the words, for I have no clear memory of what they actually were. But I am doing my best to reconstruct the *tone* that I recall. Jason Stretch's communications to his employees (me and Mrs Watson) tended to jump about a lot but were somehow without energy or final form.

I had been expecting some sort of interview but apparently the job was mine. 'Editorial and administrative responsibilities,' the ticket at the job agency had said: 'Applicants must be steady and reliable but should also be comfortable with innovative thinking.' Apart from rotten pay, this added up to the expeditions out to Island Bay; a lot of time spent sitting in an old armchair next to Mrs Watson's desk and doodling on a clipboard; and looking after the post — which meant at least one cable-car ride a day up to the Kelburn Post Office to clear the private box which Pepperell and Stretch kept there.

Then there were the leaflet runs in the afternoons. 'But nothing too arduous,' said Jason Stretch. 'The experience of walking the footpaths is going to stand you in good stead I'm sure, but there's no point in wearing yourself out.'

Here he comes, the suburban packhorse…

Some afternoons I took a sheet advertising *Pepperell's Weekly*, and sometimes I had one headed 'Astral Readings!', which started off with a whole lot of stuff about the Future and ended with an invitation to write in confidence at once, giving your date of birth.

'Send no money now but be sure to include a stamped addressed envelope for immediate return of your free Astral Interpretation. Confidentiality guaranteed. Jason M. Stretch.'

The 'Jason M. Stretch' bit was a genuine signature. Each leaflet was individually signed. Jason spent a couple of hours every morning writing his name at the foot of his promotional leaflets. Perhaps it made him feel he existed more securely, perhaps the personal touch was company policy. Perhaps it came down to the same thing.

An odd thing: I must have glimpsed Jason's signature any number of times in an afternoon, but unless I was actually looking directly at it I could never summon up an image of it. Was it large or small? Neat? Listless? A jovial flourish? What colour ink?

Come to that, as I trailed around suburban Wellington, pushing Astral Readings into the letterboxes of Kilbirnie or Thorndon or Hataitai, I couldn't quite summon up Jason himself, I couldn't get him plainly in the forefront of my mind. He was in his late thirties, I'm pretty sure, certainly a good deal older than me. His hair was shortish, fairish...but was he balding or just closely cropped? Did he wear glasses all the time, or only for reading? Now I find myself wondering if he wore glasses at all.

All I can call into being is the outline of a body and a head above a desk. There is no colour which I associate with the eyes of Jason Stretch, or with his complexion; not even with his clothing. He barely has being, for all the hundreds of times he wrote his name.

He ought to have seemed to me then — and no doubt ought to seem to me now — grotesque, colourfully Dickensian; but he is ordinary and indeterminate and unemphatic, like a dark brown desk viewed against a light brown wall, like the office furniture he sat at.

So there we were, and the truly grotesque discovery was learning that Jason's occasional references to the value of walking had a point. During January and February, he thought, I might like to lead small walking tours around Wellington. All the major cities had them, he said. There were more people than you might imagine — tourists, visitors from out of town — who *liked* to move around a city more or less at ground level, maintaining a leisurely, unhurried pace, yet all the while being kept amused and informed by knowledgeable and entertaining guides.

Jason already had two tours mapped out ($15.00 a head) and some provisional copy for the brochures. 'Historic Thorndon: a leisurely ramble through pioneer Wellington — home of prime ministers, birthplace of Katherine Mansfield.' 'Harbour City: come with us on a stroll around Wellington's busy waterfront; see views of the harbour that even Wellingtonians don't see; visit the historic Maritime Museum.'

'We'll improve the descriptive stuff; it needs to sound about two hours' worth, wouldn't you say? How's "Secret Wellington" coming along, Kevin?' 'Secret Wellington' was a walk which Jason felt we needed to have up our sleeve in case Wellington's weather made 'Historic Thorndon' and 'Harbour City' doubtful prospects. An indoor, under-cover route which stuck to Lambton Quay, Willis Street and Manners Street (for example) would be just the thing.

'Keep it in mind as you go about the city, Kevin. All the little nooks and crannies. A few historic sites. Some of the new malls and plazas. What about the new BNZ underground place? There might be something there. Check it out when you go for the post.'

So there we were, me and my prospects, sitting on the cable-car in mid-November, worrying about January and how I could possibly handle the problem of knowing enough to be able to say anything at all to tourists and out-of-towners. And what if I bumped into someone I *knew* on one of these outings? I whimpered inwardly.

'You can always take them on the cable-car,' a small inner voice whispered to me; and suddenly I knew what it meant to be able to say that your whole being glowed with pleasure. I turned over one of the airmail letters which came addressed to Jason

Stretch from Pundit Tabore, 'India's Most Famous Astrologer', of Upper Forjett Street, Bombay, India. I beamed at it in all its beauty. The flimsy brown envelope blazed out with coloured stamps. There was a woman doing gymnastic movements against a sky-blue background; against a red background a powerfully muscled man lifted weights. Five linked rings: the Olympics! But the odd thing about Pundit Tabore's letters (and here it was again) was that the stamps were always on the wrong side of the envelope. I mean, on one side of the envelope the man grunted and strained and the woman was graceful, while on the other was Jason M. Stretch's name and Wellington address.

'They always seem to get through, though,' said Mrs Watson. She was taking a break between chapters of a Communication Studies thesis. 'It must be their way of doing it. I'd love to know what that Indian's telling him.'

'Do you think he believes in it?' I said.

'Well,' said Mrs Watson, 'there must be about a dozen inquiries each week, and three or four of them end up sending the $75.00 for the full reading. I suppose they must learn something to their advantage. You need the place of birth for that, though, and the time of day as near as you can get it.'

Next morning I mentioned the cable-car to Jason.

'Well Kevin,' he said, 'let's hang fire on that one just for a little while, shall we?'

He seemed tired, but very excited.

'You know,' he said, 'an old bloke in the Catlins once told me that if you're a real bushman and it's about to rain, then you can hear the drops hitting the leaves at least a couple of minutes before the rain itself starts coming down. Even before it starts spitting, that is. Well,' he said, his voice pleased and lowered and confidential, 'I like to think I can hear people who are about to spend their money in just the same way. You can quote me on that when I'm famous.'

Of course, I am inventing the detail of Jason Stretch's words again, but not, you may be sure, out of nothing. Jason needed words like these as background and preamble to his main point, which was that he had seen on television the night before a panel discussion about nuclear winters. He had seen a way of making money.

'Horrifying. Makes you think. But it's a chance at last to combine real service to society with our own information skills. And it means real research work for you, Kevin. You'll have to move quickly, though.'

There must have been a look of reluctance on my face.

'I grew up in Balclutha,' he said, 'but here I am' — as if this would solve whatever it was that was making me so diffident.

He was jumping up and down like the man who invented hokey-pokey ice cream.

I sat in the Wellington Public Library, researching survival techniques in sub-zero temperatures. I read about the Antarctic. Mrs Watson's uncle had watched the *Terra Nova* sail from Lyttelton in 1910.

'He said it was the next best thing to Noah's Ark. I never was much interested in the dogs really, it's the ponies I feel sorry for.'

'Ponies?' I said.

NUCLEAR WINTER

War between the superpowers grows more and more likely every day!

It is well known that in the event of a nuclear exchange human life will become extinct in many areas of the planet.

Are you aware that things may be nearly as bad outside the immediate blast areas? Do you know that even a small nuclear war in the Northern Hemisphere may spell disaster in the South?

Smoke from fires burning in hundreds of cities will spread rapidly into the troposphere and stratosphere, severely limiting the amount of heat reaching the earth's surface from the sun.

A thick sooty pall. Darkness at noon. Temperatures will plummet. Imagine the cold and ice of an Antarctic winter. Many plant and animal species will be threatened with extinction.

Many communities in the Northern Hemisphere will perish from the extreme cold.

In the Southern Hemisphere some of us may survive. Within three days, scientists have forecast, concentrated jet streamers of smoke and pollutants will have poured into the atmosphere above Australia and New Zealand. Those sufficiently prepared to cope with the sudden fall in temperature may win through, but many will not — the problem is beyond the limited resources of Civil Defence. The only answer is individual initiative and forward planning.

Write at once for your 'Nuclear Winter Kit'. It contains information essential to your personal survival. Make sure you will be ready to meet all eventualities. You owe it to yourself. You owe it to your children. Send $29.95 (cheque or postal order) to 'Nuclear Winter Foundation', Box 831-240, Wellington 5. We will send your 'Nuclear Winter Kit' by return post.

There were nineteen Manchurian ponies on board the *Terra Nova*, taken to Antarctica to haul sledges. They were crammed aboard the tiny ship. 'One takes a look through the hole in the bulkhead,' wrote Scott, 'and sees a row of heads with sad, patient eyes come swinging up together from the starboard side, whilst those on the port swing back; then up come the port heads, whilst the starboard recede.' The ponies' boxes were two or three feet deep in manure when the *Terra Nova* came in sight of Antarctica.

The ponies were Manchurian, white or (a few of them) dappled grey. They cost £5 each. Captain Oates, famous for other things, was hired to look after the ponies. There are photographs taken by Ponting of the ponies aboard ship and on the ice. They are so white, the ponies, that they must often have been hard to see against the landscape they had been taken to.

There is a photograph of Oates standing on the upper deck of the *Terra Nova* with four of the ponies. Man and animals are all perfectly still, posed for the image. Among the shore photographs there is one of a pony called Chinaman with his leader, Wright. Wright faces the camera while Chinaman is in profile. There is a photograph of Oates standing with Snippets. There is Cherry-Garrard with his pony, Michael, of whom he said, 'Life was a constant source of wonder to him.' Michael is rolling on his back in the snow. Cherry-Garrard holds him on a long rein.

The ponies are greyish-white against the massive surround of ice and sky. They have coal-black eyes. The men are darker. The ponies seem to be moth-eaten; but maybe this is an effect of Ponting's photographs, or of the very rough photocopies which I made of them.

'A bit of fine tuning, but it's mostly there,' said Jason. 'We won't worry about any suburban deliveries with this one. People will be flocking into town for Christmas shopping over the next few weeks. We'll distribute directly, pass the stuff out in central Wellington.'

(Bowers records somewhere that old pony droppings, distorted by a trick of the Antarctic light, could look like a herd of cattle on the horizon.)

Oates was the man who looked after the horses. He was a taciturn man, known as the Soldier, who wrote letters to his mother. He gave two lectures on the management of horses to the men wintering over in Antarctica, ending each with a joke or anecdote. On the journey to the glacier he wrote: 'Scott realises now what awful cripples our ponies are, and carries a face like a tired sea boot in consequence.'

Of the original nineteen horses, only ten were alive when Scott and his party set out on their journey to the Pole. Some had died on board the *Terra Nova* on its journey to Antarctica. Some had died on overland training trips. Others fell from ice floes into the ocean.

Only ten survived the winter and all of these were to be shot when the sledge parties reached the Beardsmore glacier; subsequently the men would haul their own sledges. The ponies were old, at the end of their working life; they had been bought cheap by a man who knew nothing about horses. 'Poor ancient little beggar,' Bowers wrote of Chinaman. 'He ought to be a pensioner instead of finishing his days on a job of this sort.'

On 24 November 1911, Jehu was shot. His body was cut up and given to the dogs.

On 28 November, Chinaman was shot. Oates remarks, 'He was a game little devil, and must have been a goodish kind of pony fifteen years ago.'

Scott and his men were now having pony meat in their hoosh. They found it much improved.

On 1 December it was the turn of Christopher, a pony who had been 'nothing but trouble', requiring four men to hold him down whenever his harness was to be placed upon him. 'He was the only pony who did not die instantaneously,' wrote Cherry-Garrard. 'Perhaps Oates was not so calm as usual, for Chris was his own horse though such a brute. Just as Oates fired he moved, and charged into the camp with a bullet in his head. He was caught with difficulty, nearly giving Keohane a bad bite, led back and finished.'

Oates now took over the leading of Scott's pony, Snippets. Scott roved about on skis, photographing the ponies as he went.

The next pony shot was Victor. Bowers wrote: 'Good old Victor! He has always had a biscuit out of my ration, and he ate his last before the bullet sent him to his rest.'

On 4 December Michael was dispatched.

A disastrous blizzard raged for several days. On 9 December the party reached the glacier. It had been a fourteen-hour march. One member of the party later recalled the condition of the ponies, 'Their flanks heaving, their black eyes dull, shrivelled, and wasted. The poor beasts stood,' he wrote, 'with their legs stuck out in strange attitudes, mere wrecks of the beautiful little animals that we took away from New Zealand.'

The last five ponies were shot on 9 December.

When Scott and his party were dispatching the remaining ponies, more than a month of overland sledge-hauling lay ahead of them. Amundsen would reach the Pole in a matter of days. It was Oates's work with the ponies which so impressed Scott that he asked him to join the smaller team which now made the ill-fated final 'dash'.

Rajiv Gandhi stood by his mother's flaming funeral pyre, surrounded by the dignitaries of the world.

As the flames spread, India's new Prime Minister stood with his hands clasped in prayer, receiving the condolences of official mourners. Behind barriers, tens of thousands of people also mourned the death of the woman they knew as Mother India.

Nearly an hour after setting the pyre ablaze, Rajiv was still on the surrounding platform waiting according to Hindu custom for the body's head to explode.

Mourners touched their foreheads to the platform.

'Tomorrow,' said Jason Stretch, 'I think we'd better make a start on distributing these, Kevin.'

There were half a dozen big cartons of leaflets.

'I very much hope we'll need to run off a few more than this before we're finished. I think the thing will be to stick around the new shopping plazas. And we'll need to begin finalising copy for the Kit itself. How's it coming along?'

I said that I'd picked up quite a lot of material on some of the Antarctic expeditions.

'Right. And it might be worth checking with Civil Defence. They may have a few words of advice. Or tramping clubs and things like that. There must be plenty of stuff available. But see if you can get rid of a box of these first.'

I stood with my armful of leaflets outside the new AA building in Lambton Quay for forty-seven minutes before it came to me that I was never going to work up the courage to stick Nuclear Winter sheets under the noses of passing Christmas shoppers. At the same time I realised that it wasn't that I particularly disapproved of what Jason Stretch was up to. I probably did, but the real truth was that I felt silly — or was scared I would look silly. Each moment that went by, I felt a little more potentially ludicrous. From time to time someone would look at me curiously. I tried to look as though I was waiting for somebody. Help! I tried to stand there as though I wasn't there.

I wrote out my resignation on the back of a Nuclear Winter sheet and posted it to Jason's box number. 'All the best to Bob Pepperell', I added. I dumped the pile of leaflets at the end of an empty counter in the Chews Lane post office. I don't know why I should have forgotten the ponies. You grow up knowing all that stuff about Scott and Captain Oates. Oates was in charge of the ponies. That's why he was there in the first place. They called him the Soldier. I am just going outside and I may be some time.

The ponies' names were James Pigg, Bones, Michael, Snatcher, Jehu, Chinaman, Christopher, Victor, Snippets and Nobby. After I had written Jason Stretch's name and address on the envelope, I stuck the stamp on the opposite side.

I actually saw Jason about half an hour after I'd posted the letter. He was on an escalator at the new BNZ Centre. I half tried to catch his eye, but he looked straight through me — not because he was choosing to ignore me but because he wasn't quite looking at anything. I can't remember now, just a few weeks later, whether he was rising up out of the earth or descending into it.

The Poet's Wife

The poet looks at the poet's wife and says: You are my best poem. Did I ever tell you that?

The poet's wife looks at the poet. And you are my best poet, she says.

Giving a little laugh. Thinking a little thought.

The point is this, he says.

*

Years ago, before the poet's wife was, strictly speaking, the poet's wife, she wrote a little poem. She was so sick of holding open refrigerator doors. She was so sick of it all.

> dedum dedum dedum dedum
> out where Kapiti lies
> like a dark mummy on the horizon
> forever unwrapping its bandages
> into the future…

She took it to the poet, who read it aloud in that special voice of his.

When I put in the bandages, she said, I was thinking of clouds.

The poet said: Would you like to move in with me and we could talk about books and stuff?

*

She is sick of his talk of Douglas Bader's legs. She thinks: Probably some people might be impressed. But I know better.

*

Would their life together be significantly better if the poet's book royalties were put towards an annual holiday? A holiday for them both.

No it would not be better.

Last year, the poet's royalties were $43.75.

*

In fact, holidays aside, the poet has a job that brings in plenty of money. She has no idea what kind of job it is. It takes him out of the house each day, the way jobs do, and sometimes he wears walk-shorts.

*

The poet is working on his opera libretto, CARNAGE ON THE ROADS.

Don't hover! he says to his wife.

Am I hovering? says the poet's wife.

Yes, you are. *Hovering*.

Sorry, says the poet's wife.

It's just that it's extremely difficult with you hovering like that. I had something really good coming and I lost it.

*

He is actually a geography teacher and assistant careers adviser in a large North Auckland school. All he can do is warn.

*

The poet's wife reads a magazine at the hairdresser's. An article catches her eye: DANGEROUS LOVERS.

You could be looking for love in all the wrong faces. You could be ignoring the warning signs that you're romancing Mr Wrong.

I wonder, wonders the poet's wife, if he is a Don Juan or a Mother's Boy, an Obsessive Possessive or a Danger to Shipping? Or are poets different, like they say?

*

She watches a television documentary about lighthouse keepers. The loneliness. The isolation. The children taking correspondence courses. She tries to feel God in her muscles, but there is no sign of him.

*

The poet judges a poetry competition. He awards the $150.00 first prize to a poem about refrigerators written by an entrant with the pen name 'Rumpelstiltskin'. The poet receives a $500.00 judging fee. It is good the way everything is getting on to a proper professional basis he thinks. He spends the fee on personalised number plates. Now the number plates on his car say: POET 7.

Six other poets have had the number plate idea before him. They all live in Dunedin. The Dunedin school.

The poet does not live in Dunedin. He lives in his imagination.

*

The poet's wife watches a television programme about two brave elderly stroke victims. One has lost the use of her left arm, one her right. They play the piano together, each using her one good arm. They are helping each other to turn adversity into harmony.

*

Reach for the Sky. Still one of the great titles. This is only the poet's opinion, but he thinks it is a good one.

*

In the newspaper she reads about a two-headed baby which has been born in Tehran. The baby's body is outwardly almost normal, except for a third short arm. Internally, it has two hearts and four lungs, a main stomach and a sub-stomach. Each head has its own neuro system. The baby's movements are not harmonious. While one head cries, the other may be sound asleep.

*

Well, wonders the poet's wife, *am* I romancing Mr Wrong?

*

The poet's wife once had a job as a woman opening refrigerator doors. It was on television advertisements mostly, in the early days of television, though also some magazines, and sometimes there were trade displays, up on a stage, it was quite hard work actually, though it did take you round the country. This is how the poet first saw her — on television, opening a refrigerator door, in the days before colour.

*

The poet's wife hums and puts on the kettle. The poet is at a literary festival in Hamilton — reading his poems, and presenting the winning cheque to 'Rumpelstiltskin'. Soon he will be home again.

A small cloud on her horizon. What if 'Rumpelstiltskin' turns out to be a woman and not a grotesque little man? What if 'Rumpelstiltskin' is... beautiful?

*

The telephone rings. It is a journalist who is writing an article on poets' wives — from the angle of the wife, of course. He has come to feel a lot of sympathy for poets' wives in the course of his researches. He wonders if they can set up an interview?

How do you mean? says the poet's wife.

Just talk and that, says the journalist. He has a soft Irish brogue.

Will I or won't I? thinks the poet's wife.

*

He writes: 'There's a tree, one of many, of many one...' Then scores out the line with a practised scoring movement.

*

He reads Osip Mandelstam. In his sleep he cries: Nadezda!

*

She looks out of the window. Grey day. The grey before rain, the grey after rain.

The whole garden seems to sag, like a hammock sunk in the earth, slung between two stumpy lemon-trees. Neither of them exactly covered with fruit.

A simile, thinks the poet's wife.

She claps her hands in excitement. A simile!

*

He tells the pretty girl that he likes to *rescue* words — take them by the arm and lead them to some unlikely place, where they tend to look more interesting.

How do you mean? says 'Rumpelstiltskin'.

Like putting a boy from Dunedin on the streets of New York, says the poet, in a voice which indicates this is his final word on the matter.

*

Riff-raff: he cannot get the word out of his head. Dunedin riff-raff. He looks it up in the OED. Persons of a disreputable character or belonging to the lowest class of a community. Persons of no importance or social position. Unlearned rifraffe, nobodie. There were a good many riff-raff in the upper gallery. The riffe-raffe of the scribbling rascality. The Rabble or Scum of the People. Tag-rag and Long-tail. A collection of worthless persons. Odds and ends. Trumpery; trash; rubbish. A hurly-burly, a racket; a rude piece of verse.

Ah, thinks the poet, there is the title of my next book.

*

He has become interested in Douglas Bader's legs because Douglas Bader's widow wants to sell one of them. It says so in the newspaper.

*

One day the poet's wife writes a poem:

Out where Soames Island
  like a dark tape recorder
    endlessly unwinds its reels
      into the unrecorded storm

Stepping the lines down like that. Covering several pages.

*

The poet reads one of his recent poems in the foyer of the Founders Theatre in Hamilton:

> Out where Rangitoto lies
> like a dark breast
> forever bearing its nipple
> to the insatiable city…

The applause, he guesses, is somewhere between perfunctory and reluctant. He catches Rumpelstiltskin's eye. Ah! Would it be fair to call that an adoring gaze?

*

I hope he is not a TRAVELLING MAN, thinks the poet's wife.

Away from home a married man becomes a travelling man. He can take off his wedding ring. A salesman can become a company president, a company president can become a poet, a poet can become an All Black. The warning signal is seen through fog. By falling for this fellow, you are seduced by a phantom: he is no longer visible when he leaves town.

The Travelling Man can be a particularly Dangerous Lover.

*

Toynbee. The poet is on fire for her. Toynbee is Rumpelstiltskin's real name. The poet's lines flame with her being. She is the match which sets imagination alight.

He starts a little poem:

Here she comes, with her
Douglas Bader eyes,
scanning the clouds
& wild enemy skies.

But he will probably throw it away. Something tiresome about the rhyme.

*

Why only one, anyway? What has happened to the other leg? Is it lost? Is she hanging on to it for some reason? These are the sort of questions which pass through the poet's head.

*

The poet leaves his wife and goes to live with Toynbee. A big decision, but he makes it. He writes romantic passages about clouds and a few somewhat bitter lines about his wife. None of it much good. All I can do is warn, he thinks. All I can do is warn.

*

The poet's wife joins a support group for poets' wives. There are hundreds of members in the larger organisation, with branch offices all over the country.

*

She meets a woman who is now married to a stockbroker. And then there is another woman who goes around with a man who owns a whole chain of ski boutiques in the South Island. Her mind drifts off on the cloudy winds of envy…

Begorrah! (She has just remembered the Irish journalist.)

*

The poet receives an invitation to a writers' festival in Dunedin. All expenses paid. Just before the August holidays.

*

'Throw your heart over the bar, and your body will follow.'

The poet's wife reads this in a book. Because she is the kind of person who fumes and frets a lot, she keeps turning to a chapter called 'Stop Fuming and Fretting'. It tells her that she needs the peace of God in her muscles, in her joints. Then she will stop fuming and fretting.

The book says: Speak to your muscles every day and to your joints and to your nerves, saying: 'Fret not thyself' (Psalm xxxviii.i.) Think of each important muscle from head to feet, and say to each: 'The peace of God is touching you.'

*

The point is this, the poet says to her on the telephone.

But then he says nothing.

*

That wasn't you in those refrigerator ads, was it? says the journalist. Back in the Sixties when television was just starting up? I was straight off the boat. By God, you were the first good thing I saw.

*

The journalist moves in with the poet's wife. *The first good thing I saw.* His word processor comes with him. Several nights a week they go to the pub. One day the journalist writes a poem:

> Dedum dedum dedum dedum
> Out where Stewart Island lies
> like an old refrigerator
> opening and opening its door
> upon the vastness of Antarctica...

He looks her straight in the eye. So there you are then, he says. You are still a poet's wife.

*

The poet travels to Dunedin. He steps up to the podium—his eye in a fine frenzy rolling. I am the prince of clouds, he thinks, I ride out the tempest and laugh at the archer. He thinks: The Burns Fellowship. He thinks: Riff-raff. He thinks: All I can do is warn.

*

They make love, a strenuous bout.

Afterwards, the poet's wife draws a rectangle; in it she draws two lines which intersect to form a cross. Guess what it is, she says.

A window? says the journalist.

No.

A parcel?

No.

What, then?

A short story, she says. With a trick ending.

*

The poet's wife sits at the word processor. Her fingers fly over the keys. Now what is that? A simile? Of course not. Perhaps a cliché? Or — an image of transcendence?

*

The poet explains how he used to be fascinated by the idea of a poop deck — the phrase itself seemed naughty. He imagined a deck covered in…well, not to put too fine a point on it…poop. But looking back…looking back, he can see the first stirrings of the poet there. That interest in language — the young boy sniggering in the playground — in love with the sea, in love with his native tongue…

Stop me, he says, if this is boring you. Or if it isn't the sort of thing you want.

No, says the *Landfall* interviewer. No not at all. She smiles behind her hand.

*

The journalist stands on the roof of the house. For a while he stares down at the garden: one rhododendron, two lemon-trees. Other houses in the distance. Is he going to jump? Of course not. He is going to fall. My beautiful one! he cries. My icebox girl! My mistress of the lonely voice…

Highlights

They are in Rotorua, but the Bellevue no longer has a view and is also double-booked. The apologetic girl at the desk is professionally reassuring. He leaves his mother in the car and hovers in the lobby while she phones around. Out on Fenton Street motels push and jostle for room. Belaire, Boulevard, Matador, Sulphur City, Rob Roy, Pineland, Ascot, Forest Court, Nikau Lodge... It will be all right.

Each time she puts the phone down the girl looks across and smiles to indicate she will try again. Eventually she beckons him over and asks would he like her to try one of the big hotels. Her friend at the Kiwi Panorama has reminded her about the August school holiday family packages. It might even be cheaper than a motel. As long as you eat out, she adds.

They can have three nights at the Randwick International (room rate $75.00), but no more because of the incoming police convention.

'It's enough, though, isn't it,' says his mother through the car window. She looks tired yet determined, she talks between bites of a tomato sandwich. 'Let's have the nights they can give us. We'll just do the main things, and then you take me home, Robert.'

He steps out on to their room's small balcony. The imitation Spanish railing curls up to hip-level. He blinks in the pale mid-afternoon sunshine. Which way is the lake? Across the road is what looks like an abandoned motel complex — a long, low, L-shaped structure made of pink and green tinted concrete blocks. The roadside windows are boarded up, there are crates of empty bottles stacked outside. A man squats on the roof, painting it a gunmetal grey.

He turns back inside where his mother sits on the huge bed among colour brochures. He looks inside the fridge unit, which is well stocked with expensive juices and miniatures.

'I want to do the highlights, Robert. Two things tomorrow and something on Thursday.'

'It's your treat,' he says. 'Your birthday.'

She has just turned seventy-five.

'We'll have to go to the mud pool place,' she says. 'Then you choose one thing and I'll choose one.'

He leaves her to it. In the corridor he is passed by several small children, wet and wrapped in pink towels, running ahead of a parent. A blackboard in the lobby bears the chalk inscription, *Kids! Superman 2 in video lounge 4.30*. At the desk a man who looks like an airline steward is issuing towels.

He turns left through french windows and finds himself in a spacious courtyard. Bamboo clumps, shrubs and patio tables. Children wriggle at the shallow end of a curved swimming pool. At the deep end men and women float against the edge, their arms along the railings like boxers resting between rounds.

A Chinese woman in a straw hat sits disconsolately in a smaller, square pool. A notice indicates that it is a spa pool but that the agitator is out of order. A third pool, even smaller — it might hold two people at a pinch — gives off a sulphurous stench. Robert touches his fingers into the water and quickly lifts them away. The heat is surprising. He reads a long notice which has two paragraphs about the health-giving qualities of the water and two about the precautions which the hotel would like to recommend because of possible dangers to health.

Next morning they park the car in Tryon Street. His mother makes her way through the drizzle towards a little cluster of souvenir shops. In the window of the shop she enters, a fat kiwi lazes in a deckchair, staring through sunglasses at a blue ocean horizon. A New Zealand flag waves above him. At his feet a handwritten sign says, *Customers wanted, please apply in shop*.

His mother is picking up and putting down items made from

paua shell. Key-rings, ashtrays, coasters, lucky horseshoes, nail clippers, a game of noughts and crosses.

'Aren't they *clever,*' she says. The shop is an adventure.

On the wall behind her is a large poster, a map which shows New Zealand grown astonishingly large, mainly because Australia has been drawn as a tiny island off to the left. Perhaps he should get it for Peter — it might look amusing in a Sydney flat.

'Of course, you can just pick them up at the beach,' his mother says.

It might not be the right sort of thing. People prefer to make their own jokes. He didn't think he knew his son especially well. He didn't know what amused him really. But he ought to find something. He had felt absurd embarrassment at the airport when he realised he had no farewell gift, and then had felt silly for feeling he ought to have one. Only after Peter had gone through immigration did he notice the airport gift shop, its mugs with kiwis, its shirts with sheep. But he had driven back to Browns Bay.

On a shelf in front of him are rulers and chessboards made of native woods. There is a pencil case, like the one he was given when he started primary school, which he decides to buy. He will also buy some sachets of 'Miracle Mud — from the natural boiling pools in New Zealand's "Thermal Wonderland"'.

'Thank you, sir,' says the assistant.

'That's a good one,' his mother says. She is looking at a sign which says, *We have trained our souvenirs not to touch children; please train your children not to touch the souvenirs.* She does not buy anything.

A pale blue plastic comb is floating in a hot pool called Te Weranga — 'the place where someone was burned'. The drizzle comes and goes. They keep their umbrellas up.

His mother has a pair of poi looped around her neck. They look like bulbs of garlic, except that they are orange. She bought them ten minutes ago from a ten-year-old girl. She has taken a photograph of the girl, standing next to Robert, in front of her stall. A condition of sale.

They come to the model pa but go quickly across to the carving centre where they can be out of the rain. This is also the main entrance to Whakarewarewa. Coaches are parked in the distance.

They join a line of people moving slowly along a walkway which skirts the outside of the carving workshop, a room marginally larger than their hotel bedroom. Three men tap with chisels, working on pieces which are at different stages of completion. One piece is barely begun — a length of wood with lines marked on the surface. The trainee carvers are all young, about Peter's age. From time to time they break off and stare at the piece on which they are working. It is hard to tell if they are inventing or remembering.

Out in the vestibule a young man in blue shorts and red jandals points with proprietorial pride at a carved wall panel. He must have made it. But the friend with him has the same gaze of satisfied ownership.

Where is his mother? Robert scans the tour groups who are gathered around women working with flax and feathers. 'And so we are spreading knowledge of these ancient arts,' a guide says. His mother has gone through into the souvenir area.

She has bought six copies of a postcard showing five small Maori boys, each naked, each poking out his tongue, each making a haka gesture with one hand while the other hand modestly covers (or clutches?) his genitals. She takes them out of the packet to show him.

Below the model pa the route loops past a Kiwi Nocturnal House. *Night conditions exist. Keep silent. No smoking. No photos.*

He follows his mother through two sets of doors and enters a dark curve crammed with bodies. There is loud, excited talking and a smell of dampness. Children are tapping on the glass window.

'Here it is,' cries a man. 'Over here!'

Robert looks but can see nothing. Dark branches.

'Here it is,' cries a voice like his mother's. 'Over here!'

He looks but can see neither the kiwi nor his mother.

Ten minutes later they are walking past the geysers. Are they playing? Steam drifts indistinctly through the rain. They walk back down through the white raised tombs of the small Catholic cemetery, cross a bridge and pass out through the archway which commemorates the dead.

> It is the proud claim of the Tuhourangi people that on the outbreak of the Second World War all the men in the village between the age of 16 and 60 years enlisted for overseas service. The memorial arch at the entrance to Whaka tells the story of their contribution to the wargod, Tumatauenga.

'Twenty-five *naughty* boys,' his mother says in the car, admiring her postcards. 'Did you see these, Robert?'

Then she says, 'I never liked the way your father put his tongue in my ear.'

Robert does not remember his father, who was in the engine room of the *Achilles* and died at sea two days out from Auckland. It had been a heart attack. 21 February 1940. The *Achilles* was sailing home to a heroes' welcome after the Battle of the River Plate. Robert's mother had travelled all the way to Auckland to be among the 100,000 people gathered to cheer the ship's company as they marched up Queen Street. She had waited in the crowd, unaware of her husband's death. Much later, she seemed to remember the thrill of the parade more vividly than her subsequent distress. She was interested in the grief but no longer felt it. Robert had been two. He had been left with some people in Dunedin.

'One thing at least is certain,' wrote Captain Parry, commander of the *Achilles*. 'The continued enthusiasm and cheerfulness, both in dull moments and in more exciting ones, of a predominantly New Zealand ship's company has been a revelation, and for four anxious days an inspiration to one who was bred and born in the Old Country. Though many weary and anxious times lie ahead, he feels complete confidence that such men cannot fail to win the final victory.'

Robert has no memory of his father — except for an impression, refined over many years, of what must once have been a dream. He is in a rowing boat with a smiling man in naval uniform. They are on a lake, the day is nearly over. The man explains that they are going to the island to see how the other children are getting on. 'Nearly there,' he sometimes says, 'nearly there.' Darkness and moonlight drip from his oars.

They drive quickly around the Government Gardens but do not leave the car. Robert's mother has run out of film. He parks the car on one of the shopping streets and dashes through rain towards a doorway.

He is in a colourful shop. A big man behind the counter is wearing an Argentine rugby jersey. It is too small for him. He is beef and teeth, a puma snarls beneath his collar. 'Ours is a speciality emphasis,' he says. He is sorry. Rosettes, yes, ties, replica jerseys, novelty cutlery — but no films. Behind him a sign says, *Shoplifters get court*. 'Up the road,' he says, and gestures up the road.

Robert tells his mother they will get a film at Rainbow & Fairy Springs. This is the tourist attraction he has picked out. First, though, they lunch at Springs Cottage. A filled roll for Robert, and a cream bun which seems to taste of chicken; a Devonshire tea for his mother. The rain comes and goes. Cars drive away, others pull up.

Entering Rainbow Springs they pass through another souvenir area. They get a film, then go on and gaze at pools of fish. They walk along bush trails, gazing from bridges and platforms, looking through underwater viewing windows. Rainbow-striped umbrellas jostle above the heads of the visitors. Children tug and quarrel beneath them, clutching bags of fish-food. There is another kiwi house, which Robert decides not to enter. He tells his mother he will wait for her in the souvenir shop. Rain on the gravel walkways.

He decides to buy another pencil case.

'I saw it,' says his mother. 'What do you want another one of those for?'

'I thought I might send it to Peter.'

'The time for that,' says his mother, 'was when she took him off.'

'She' is his ex-wife, Lorraine. Robert is Lorraine's ex-husband. Peter, he supposes, is his ex-son.

'It's just sentimental,' he says. 'Something I remember. A bit like your clothes-pegs.'

Robert is changing the subject. On her mantelpiece his mother keeps seven clothes-pegs. She won them when 'It's in the Bag' came to Lumsden. She should have taken the money.

Robert can still remember the entry for Lumsden in *Wise's New Zealand Index* ('every place in New Zealand, 9th edition'). He once learned it by heart. He wrote it out in a letter to his Australian penfriend.

> A town district and railway junction, on Oreti River; 50 miles north from Invercargill. Southland County. Sheep and dairy farming. Excellent trout fishing in Oreti River and good shooting. Splendid roads for motoring. Three good hotels. Post, telegraph, and money order office. Population, 510. The old name of this place was The Elbow.

Robert's mother worked as a housemaid-waitress at the Railway Hotel. 'Not live-in,' she occasionally said. She and Robert had their evening meal there, even on nights she wasn't working. It was always a roast, they always walked home together afterwards.

Robert's mother buys a teatowel with a spray of pohutukawa on it. She would like to go back to the Randwick now for a rest. Last night they ate at Pizza Hut. Tonight they are going to eat at McDonald's.

They are early at the Agrodome, a good half-hour before the morning show begins. They wander about in the sheepskin shop, occasionally peering out at the grey weather. Robert's mother picks up handknitted jerseys, exclaiming at the prices.

Robert browses in a booklet, *New Zealand and Its Sheep*, by Godfrey Bowen. Godfrey Bowen is a champion shearer who helped found the Agrodome. He writes lyrically of the farmers and shepherds of the world. They know no strikes, their work is like a calling. He speaks, too, of 'Mum', the farmer's wife. She feeds the family, fixes a broken garage door, drives the tractor, takes telephone messages. She makes the farmhouse a haven of peace.

Robert's mother tugs him into the hall. She wants a seat at the front. The hall fills up behind them.

'Is there anybody here from Scotland?' calls the bush-singleted compère. 'What about Ireland? Spain? The Old Country?'

One by one he calls off the nations of the earth.

'Is there anybody here from the South Island?' Robert's mother makes a faint noise in her throat, half lifting a hand. Roars of self-acclaim come from the back rows.

'Is there anybody here from Japan?' Silence greets this query, although Robert can see a party of Japanese tourists on the other side of the aisle. In fact one has got to his feet now, but only to take a photograph.

'Welcome one and all,' says the compère, 'whatever part of this great planet you hail from.' He explains that his name is Colin, and that the parade of rams will now take place. A taped commentary by Godfrey Bowen will accompany the presentation. Then he will shear a sheep.

There are nineteen rams, each representing a different breed. One by one they clatter into position on a set of tiered ramps, tempted by some sort of granulated feed in a canister whose lid is released by a pretty girl. As each ram begins snuffling in its canister, she chains it in place. Meanwhile Godfrey Bowen declares the breeds and countries of origin, adding something about the history and characteristics of each breed. The breeds of ram seem to be named after English towns and counties: Lincoln, Leicester, Suffolk, Dorset. The rams have their own names, too. Trotting one by one from opposite sides of the stage to be locked into position by the pretty girl come Rajah, Duke, Monarch, Sultan, Sambo. A bored merino ram called Prince has pride of place at the top of the pyramid.

Colin spreads his arms. People stand to take photographs. Others applaud.

Colin reaches into a pen and drags out a ewe. He wrestles it to its back. 'Wool,' he says. 'As old as time, as modern as tomorrow.'

As he shears, he calls out interesting facts. New Zealand leads the world in grasslands farming. Revolutionary techniques in top-dressing and pasture control mean that grass will grow for eleven months in most parts of the country. There are thirty sheep for each man, woman and child in New Zealand. There are seventy million sheep all told, of which fifty million are breeding ewes — 'like this lady here.'

There is an in-gasping moan from some members of the audience as a bright fleck of blood appears on the ewe's belly. Then there is a sprinkling of applause. Flashlights flash. The ewe is released into the rainy paddocks.

Colin raises the cloudy fleece above his head.

'Just like peeling a banana,' he says. 'I can tell you, ladies and gentlemen, the shearer works fast. Any decent sort of shearer would get through, oh, 300-350 sheep a day. And that's currently at about 61 cents a fleece around these parts.'

Because of the rain there will be no sheepdog demonstration, but a dog called Smoko bounds up the backs of the rams, leaping from one to another until he settles barking on the back of Prince the merino. Prince looks bored and sits down. The pretty girl tugs him to his feet. There will now be a period for formal photographs. The man Colin, the dog Smoko, and the ram Prince will be only too happy to pose with members of the audience. A queue quickly forms. Robert's mother insists that he join it. 'Smile,' she says.

Robert relaxes in the pool at the Randwick, thinking vaguely that he still has not seen the lake. His mother is lying down in their room, pleased with the Agrodome. 'The best of the lot,' she has decided. 'They all have their personalities, don't they?' She means the rams.

The pool is empty. The children and their parents have gone. A few pink abandoned towels. Tomorrow the police will come. Robert remembers something Peter told him over their drink in the airport bar. He was trying to bring to mind a moment he could only half recall from childhood. Robert had taken him to the local swimming pool and had cradled him all the way from one side of the deep end to the other. It was the first time he had been in at the deep end.

Robert cannot remember the occasion. Perhaps it had been a friend of Lorraine's, though he took care not to make the suggestion to Peter. It is impossible to know how much an experience means to another person. What will his mother remember about Rotorua?

(In ten days' time Robert's mother will send him a colour photograph. On the back will be written, in her careful hand: *Robert and his 'royal friend'*. Prince's look of boredom will be exactly as Robert remembers. Robert's face will show an almost unimaginable happiness.)

Meantime there is the problem of where to eat. Perhaps they will try a hangi at one of the hotels. He floats on his back. He is pleased with himself: by accident he has stolen Godfrey Bowen's book about New Zealand sheep. It is in the car glovebox. 'The next book I write will be of my life, when I can go into more detail.'

A memory comes to him, unbidden, of his mother at the big wooden table in the kitchen at Lumsden. Sometimes she would earn extra income by colour-tinting the aerial photographs taken by one of the local top-dressing pilots. They were large black-and-white images, each with a farmhouse at the centre. Eventually they would hang in the farmhouses they represented.

The tiny brushes and little bottles of water-colours are spread out around her. Her name is Eileen Taylor. Her hand dips and hovers, she works with patience and precision. She does the roofs of houses and outbuildings first — red or green, sometimes orange. Then she colours the farm roads a putty yellow.

Picking out the highlights, it is called. Stands of pine and macrocarpa windbreaks are tinted green, creeks and ponds become an unreal blue. The paddocks are left grey, stretching out to the edges of the frame.

Ventriloquial

The Hermit of Peking

The woman from the Historic Places Trust is nervous. Her name is Sarah. She chatters on about chopsticks, MSG, hyperactive children, she has two herself, she should know. Would the magazine contemplate a piece on turn-of-the-century sawmills? Or, and granted this goes a little beyond her own area of expertise, something on the old macrocarpa wind-breaks of Southland?

I spin the revolving warmer and take a little more Stir-fried Broccoli with Hoisin Sauce, perhaps just another helping of Drunken Chicken. I make a mental note to be fair. This is Sarah's first magazine lunch, and naturally enough she is trying too hard. Also, my foot is stroking her leg.

The talk comes round to racehorses. Racehorses or something similar is often the way of it. Tom Mendoza, our bloodstock correspondent, offers the thought that there are an awful lot of horses around at the moment which seemed to be named after artists. Forget all those nags called Monet or Van Gogh across in Europe. What puzzles me, says Tom, is that so many of our own folk, owners and trainers, are going the same way. So are we coming of age in a cultural sense then? Or is this further evidence of the derivative nature of our way of life? Once it was Phar Lap and Cardigan Bay; now it is Woollaston, who must, incidentally, stand not a bad chance in the Caulfield Cup...And Rita Angus, well there you're starting to talk household names...

Jimmy Kwok, proprietor of this fine establishment, comes across to ask if everything is to our satisfaction. He cannot, poor man, entirely conceal his disappointment. Like others, he had expected to see Richard Hadlee at our table. Alas, Christchurch airport has been closed for two days by an unacceptable level of bird-strikes. Never mind, we have two middle-ranking Cabinet Ministers, a knight from the Business Roundtable, someone from Avalon, a country-and-western singer called Hank Mushroom, and the University Vice-Chancellor, who is also a physicist of consequence. He flies around the world discoursing on a shadow universe of dark matter...electromagnetic whispers...the place where particle physics and astrophysics join hands and speak to us...The V-C has taken a liking to the Stewed Pork with Fermented Beancurd and Taro — just as well since no one else is keen to pursue it beyond the first mouthful and, as usual at the Hermit of Peking, there are Jimmy Kwok's feelings to bear in mind.

I ask Sarah to come back to our handsome harbourfront tower block and elaborate her ideas a little. She bites her lower lip, toys with her rice. Hank Mushroom begins to describe his trip to Nashville. The place defies description really...

I try to listen. But there is nothing much for us here.

Coastal Flashback

When I was a boy I thought that throwing your voice meant precisely that. The books I read were full of heroes who saved the day by cleverly throwing their voices. All right Cunningham! Drop the gun! Overpowering villains was a routine exercise, you simply distracted them first. It was not so much that you talked without moving your lips, although that must have been important. The crucial thing was to actually make your voice come from some distant object...a vase of flowers across the room, or a button jar beside your mother's elbow, or the ancient great-aunt who has come to stay for a while and is now asleep in the corner — her face as pale as electricity, and her whole body giving off that fishy smell which sometimes signals an electrical fault.

I show my aunt my bag of milk bottle tops. Silver, she says. Are you a good boy, Hugo?

And when Aunt wakes, she is neither rich nor married. She is in this awful house, she has been here three years now, how did that happen? A boy in the corner is putting on a coat with a strip of reflector tape on the back; he is about to go out the door and get on his bicycle and ride off down the road to wherever it is a boy like him might go at this time of night. Don't let your uncle come and get me, cries my aunt. We explain, for the umpteenth time, that he has been dead for years. But he can *materialise*, she says. Can't you *see*?

Aunt sinks back into her chair. There is that fishy smell again. Down on the beach the gang members are giving their German shepherds a run on the sand. They throw sticks for them, dash into the surf a bit, things like that. I wheel my bicycle carefully through the twilight.

Pioneer Women's Hall

First our donation at the door. The suggested amount is $25.00. Quite usual, Frank tells me. We are in the kichen/dining-room of the Pioneer Women's Hall. There is a sink just to our left; a white Zip hangs above it. Are there more of us here? Why yes. There are several elderly persons, widows and widowers, none of them known to me. No familiar faces — although isn't that Josephine the Spanish dancer on her knees at the front erecting her portable wooden floor? Frank whispers that there will not, of course, be any Spanish dancing; Josephine is actually related to the medium in some way, cousins he thinks. We settle back and wait.

Domestic Interior

Charles Laughton, the young Maori novelist, rings me up at home. I am in bed with Sarah. We ran a paragraph on him in the magazine gossip column about three months ago and he has plagued us ever since. He wants something more substantial. When are you sending that reporter round, says Charles Laughton. When we have space on the schedule, I say. Well, Hugo, people want to know about me, he says, I get approached on the street, I think you should do me soon. He begins to describe a short story he is about to start work on. It is written from the point of view of a boy from the East Coast travelling in Canada in the late nineteenth century. The story has a working title: 'Tolaga Bay: The Days of Sail'.

Sarah begins to do something interesting to the lower part of my body while Charles Laughton goes on with his story. I sigh into the telephone. It has been a surprising few weeks. It turns out that Sarah is my neighbour, she lives just beyond the clematis and honeysuckle. She and her husband moved in about six months ago. Frank and Sarah Husband. I hadn't even noticed the departure of the previous neighbours. Frank and Sarah Husband have no children. So what Sarah said at the Hermit of Peking was a spur of the moment invention. I find this unreliability only makes her more attractive. Frank works in the Department of Social Welfare. He is happy for Sarah to lead an interesting life, even the part of it that now involves me. He watches her vanish through the honeysuckle... a smile hovers on his lips... he makes the noise of an aeroplane taking off.

Frank Husband is a ventriloquist. He talks to his dummy, Disraeli, late into the evening. Voices are raised in argument, neither of them Sarah's. Frank watches videos; he has a fine Tarzan collection. I have told Sarah how keen I am to meet him: I always wanted to be able to throw my voice when I was a boy. Maybe drinks one evening?

I make my excuses to Charles Laughton. In fact, I tell him that it sounds as if he has the makings of a whole *novel* there. I cut him off halfway through the Inuit Ceremony of Welcome.

Sixteenth Floor

The Thursday post lands on my desk, its thump shaking the tower block. Here they are, the latest issues of *Esquire, Vogue, Penthouse, Tatler, Paris Match, Watchtower, The Face, Agricultural Machinery, Spare Rib, Oomph!, Indecent Assault, Sorcerer, Mädchen, Now/Then, Ectoplasm, Soviet Weekly, Grendel's Mother, The New Yorker, Nonetheless, Health and Beauty, Contretemps, Turf Digest, Studio International.* A modest queue has formed. I pass the magazines out to appropriate members of staff. Each goes off to comb through the pages, seeking that special piece which may meet the exacting requirements of local adaptation.

I give Sarah the latest issue of *Knave* and wink at her. And how is the piece on macrocarpa windbreaks coming along, I ask our latest staff writer. Astonishingly, she replies that she needs to travel to Southland *with* the photographer, not just write second-hand captions after seeing the contacts. Can I not get that into my head? And what about the other project? She has told me several times now about Thomas Barnhill and the trees he planted at Castle Rock station to commemorate troop dispositions at Waterloo. Have I come to a decision? Maybe she is mistaken, but she thought I was the editor.

I sigh, and stare out at the squid boats in the harbour. Sarah Husband is by no means one of those workers who kneels under the boss's desk. Though of course she would probably not refuse if asked.

Meanwhile, in the large open-plan offices on the floors below, work goes on. Lists are compiled, the telephones are busy. The lunch invitations go out, the subscription copies pour in. The newest clerical assistant goes out to buy more scissors. It is all part of our ceaseless search for new ideas.

Rainbow Warrior

Cushions around a low table, same old blackboard menu. Did we really mean to invite *two* heart surgeons? I remember posting out the invitation to the immediate past-president of Federated Farmers myself. And the others all make some sort of sense — the society astrologer, Josephine from the Spanish Dancing Academy, the politician who wants to privatise the prison services, the English Department lecturer who turns out to be New Zealand contributing editor of *Now/Then*. Don't we see that one from time to time, I say. Interesting graphics, is that the one?

The man from the English Department wears a T-shirt which says 'Make Me An Offer'. He is balding and incomprehensible; he talks and his lips don't move. He is keen to work up a piece on the death of Norman Kirk. In rhetorical terms, he declares, that whole event was a discourse substitute, wasn't it? He waits for his words to sink in. But will it make a punchy 1,500-word article, front of book, with visual potential? I fear not.

Talk among our staffers, also Josephine and the astrologer, turns to Charles Laughton. He is doing well, despite his name. Does the poor man *know?* Still, the way Fletcher Challenge snapped him up as writer in residence... And just the other week there was that profile in the *Listener*, quite well done though hardly enough to halt the circulation slide.

Well, says the man from the English Department, he makes it clear that he is being patient: What *happens* when we create discourse?

But here is the founding editor of *The Dictionary of New Zealand Biography*, we rise to greet him, distinguished man with a pipe, better late than never. We pour him a bowl of muesli. Now tell me, says the society astrologer, would you for argument's sake put someone like Charles Laughton in this book of yours? The case doesn't arise, says the editor of the *DNZB*, he isn't dead yet. Then he adds, puffing serenely: We *are* thinking seriously about Kupe.

Ye gods!

Kiri Te Kanawa has called in sick, the Everly Brothers are

delayed in Manila, Colin Meads and Michael Joseph Savage have failed to answer their letters. The man from the English Department puts a ten-dollar note on the table and gets to his feet. I ate very little, he says. I just picked at my salad. He looks pleased — as if we have failed some sort of test…

Next Tuesday the John Wayne Chophouse, then maybe the Rive Gauche or the Rumbling Frog.

Next Door

Sarah is in the master bedroom, the door closed. She has been back from the South Island a fortnight now, working and reworking her macrocarpa piece. Frank watches *Greyfriars Bobby* with the sound down. I keep him company.

You're talking, says Frank, about distant voice technique.

He makes the noise of a bath emptying; the sound seems to come from the ceiling. He picks up the telephone. Get me Paul Keating. Keating comes on the line. Frank has a long chat with him about Australian foreign policy, and Keating agrees to most of Frank's suggested initiatives — leasing Tasmania to the French, invasion of Burma, night landings on the Malvinas. I can hear the voice, as clear as day: sleek and nasal, yet metallic down the line.

Talk to you later, says Frank. Catch you Frank, says Keating.

Sarah calls from the bedroom: Hugo! Can I ask you something?

I go through. What is it? says Sarah.

I thought you called, I say. Can I help or something?

Not me, she says, no way, I'm doing perfectly well, thank you.

Frank flicks off the video. So there are two crucial elements, he tells me. First: the gift of mimicry, either you have it or you don't. Second: breath control, with particular regard to techniques of drone and rib reserve.

He asks me to consider a diagram of the human vocal and respiratory mechanism.

I find it hard to pay attention. There is a distressed bird flying around the room. How did it get in? It hits the window, batters the glass, repeatedly, drops to the floor. I can hear the feeble beating of wings on carpet. Now a car pulls up in the street. A door slams: footsteps, a woman's voice, a single piercing scream. I race to the front door and fling it open. Nothing. Black empty night.

Frank Husband comes and stands beside me. Back in the house Sarah makes faint noises of sexual arousal. Frank's teeth flash in the moonlight. The ventriloquial effect, he says.

Pioneer Women's Hall

Flickering candlelight. Darkness of the other side. The Zip floats eerily above the sink, like ectoplasm. The man in the blue cardigan writhes between two women.

I have a message for someone in this room. You go.

Mr Mikes stops writhing; he sits upright in his wooden chair. His arms are stretched horizontally: each woman holds a wrist. They might be nurses taking his pulse. One of them is Josephine.

You go?

Frank nudges me. Wake up Hugo!

Yes, I say, my name is Hugo. The message might be for me.

What is it dear, says Josephine. She inclines her head towards Mr Mikes. Hugo is here; have you a message for him?

Aunt Beattie...says that...she has found...happiness. Uncle Graham is here...they are together...again. She says...there is now...and there is...then...

My Aunt Beattie? My Uncle Graham?

She's gone, says Josephine. I'm sorry.

My Aunt Beattie?

Can we have Peter now, please? says Josephine. She and the other woman seem to tighten their grip on Mr Mikes' wrists.

Here we go, Frank whispers.

I open my notebook and lean forward.

Sixteenth Floor

Occasionally even I am astonished by the magazine's success. I pinch myself to see if it is all true. Ouch! Of course I was confident at the outset. We had put a good little team together, the right mix of skills and personalities: those who like to move the ball out quickly along the line, those who prefer to make a jinking little run. We have a circulation of 90,000 copies per issue, fully audited, steadily rising. A good 10,000 more with a Royal cover story. Not bad for something launched on hope and a shoestring just twenty-one months ago. Not bad, as I will probably observe in our birthday editorial, for a little country at the bottom of the South Pacific.

Advertisers clamour for space; we cannot meet the demand. Nearly 1,000 copies of each issue go to overseas subscribers eager to keep up with what goes on in our corner of the world.

On my desk, the latest titles mount up: *Harper's & Queen, Business Traveller, Cycling World, Women in Management, Country Life, Moroccan Zero, New Scientist, Marauder, Time, Newsweek, Soldier of Fortune, New Left Review, Angiospore,* the *Illustrated London News, Rasta!,* the *Wall Street Journal, Rough Trade, Deneuve,* the *Joseph Conrad Newsletter.* I try to sort them into some semblance of order. The clock ticks on; the queue begins to form at my door.

Bad Dream: Domestic Interior

Hugo, says Frank, meet Hugo. Frank has brought his dummy across to say hello. The dummy's eyebrows are made of black felt; the rest of his head is painted, even the hair. The mouth can move: the middle of the chin drops away when Frank operates a lever in the dummy's back.

That's a real coincidence, I say, the names being the same. But I thought his name was Disraeli…

You've been talking to Sarah, says Hugo. How well the two of you have lasted. But Sarah is very much out of touch now. We've been thinking of this particular name change for quite some time, haven't we Frank?

Frank nods. His mouth drops open.

Arthur Prince and Sailor Jim. Edgar Bergen and Charlie McCarthy. Peter Brough and Archie Andrews. Shari Lewis and Lamb Chop. Paul Winchall and Knucklehead Smiff. Frank Husband and Hugo.

Next Door Flashback

Frank and I are watching a video. I wonder aloud, if I will ever get to meet his ventriloquial doll. Frank says that Disraeli is shy, he likes to keep himself to himself. But I know that later tonight, after I have gone home — maybe with Sarah, more likely by myself — voices will be raised, Frank and Disraeli will discuss the day's events, maybe even discuss me.

Sarah sits through at the big kitchen table, with shots of windbreaks spread out around her. Some of them are very fine, I have to acknowledge. The movie Frank and I are watching is an old one: *Devil Doll*. It stars a ventriloquist called Vorelli whose dummy, Hugo, becomes a monster. Hugo is locked in a cage every night.

Most of it is farcical; very occasionally there is that authentic note of chill.

Sixteenth Floor

Yes? I look up from my notes on the Korean Peace Dam. Oh, it's you.

Sarah stands in the doorway. She has come to hand in her final assignment: a report on the medieval jousting tournament in Tauranga.

Hugo, she says, it was too good to last. You must have known it was time.

I toy with my pen. I think: Sarah, I have seen you flabbergasted, rattled, lost for words; I have seen you gasping on my oatmeal carpet.

By the time I look up from my thoughts, Sarah has slipped out, en route to her new job at Radio New Zealand. But somewhere in North Korea, the proposed Peace Dam is still on the drawing board. The plan apparently involves the construction of a giant earth dam, with a corresponding mass of water backed up behind it, in a valley near the border. The threat is silent, but real enough. Should the water be released, within minutes the National Assembly Building in Seoul will be drowned. Naturally, the Government of South Korea has begun to plan its own dam; it will face the North Korean dam.

They grow slowly in the mind: the two giant walls of compacted earth, each with a vast lake spreading out behind it. Perhaps there will be pleasure boats and water-skiing. And, between the two dams, lush market gardens.

I am working my way towards the magazine's birthday editorial. It is still several issues off, but it needs to be just right. So, I have a striking metaphor, one which grows in the mind; but where will it take me? East-West relations? New Zealand's own hydro-electric schemes? The general state of preparedness of Civil Defence? I want to get some bridge, too, into the magazine itself. I wonder if I could praise Charles Laughton's new play — the one now touring China, in which all the people of the whanau go about on crutches? The dazzling symbolism, the theatrical coup, needs to be acknowledged; but maybe there is some greater lesson here? Might not the young playwright's perception apply to *all* the peoples of Aotearoa/New Zealand? Etc. And then maybe some further words about a shared future — with the magazine, its happy marriage of idealism and experience, etc., playing its own small part in building the nation of the future. Like the future, we hope to be around for some time yet.

My desk sags under the weight of *Cosmopolitan, Harper's Bazaar, National Geographic, Matelot, Oggi, Chiffonier, Stand Clear of the Moving Handrail, PN Review, People's Friend, Elle, City Limits, Mayfair, Gibbon's Stamp Monthly, Seance, This Way Up, High Society, Junior Alchemist, The*

Lady, Cropdusting Monthly, Astrolabe, Leprosy Review, Badminton Today.

After Sarah told me, I said to Frank, Frank, I'm sorry, let me know if there's anything...

She's not leaving me, Hugo, Frank replied. Just you.

Pioneer Women's Hall

Mr Mikes pants and moans, jerking from his shoulders. I could swear he has an erection...the light makes it difficult to tell. He wails and snorts, his voice makes a smothered sound.

Yes Peter, says Josephine. Is that you now, dear? Hello? Peter?

Mr Mikes pulls his arms free. He sits with his fists clenched in front of him like a boxer, sparring with the empty air.

Oh, she says, it's Daniel. Daniel, can we please have Peter?

Mr Mikes slumps in his chair. The spirits drift down the long corridor of his body. The women take up his wrists again.

Mr Mikes says: Peg.

Hello Peter, says Josephine. Can you hear me?

Mr Mikes nods; his upper body seems to force the movement out. He says: Goodness gracious me.

For a moment he slumps. Then he straightens, the women hold him. Now his voice is American. Balham, he announces, Gateway to the South!

Mr Mikes does the whole Peter Sellers sketch: word-perfect, voice-perfect. He carves the little holes in the tops of toothbrushes. There is honey still for tea. Then he goes straight into Sellers doing Olivier doing 'A Hard Day's Night'. Each word is cold, clipped, separate.

What next? We hold our breath.

But Mr Mikes falls forward. He has plummeted from his trance, he gives off a fishy smell. The women help him from the room.

Staggering, says Frank. What do you think, Hugo?

I do not know what to think. But I am willing to be persuaded there is a feature here, if only we can get the illustrations right. I look at my notebook. I have written the words, 'Now then'.

Tandoori Heaven

Frank Sinatra has failed to show. But we were aiming high there. Hone Tuwhare has sent an apology — a terse, handwritten note, free verse, already safe in the archive. The Deputy Prime Minister is opening a Rollerdrome in Wanganui. There has been an acceptance from the Director of the SIS. But apparently he is sitting at another table.

Still, Frank Husband is here — minus Disraeli, who is unwell. Frank is angling, not very subtly, for the recently advertised job of features editor. He is sick of the Department of Social Welfare. First things first, I say to him. Let's see what you can do with the ventriloquism piece, you need some sort of track record. He nods his head but clearly isn't happy.

One of the country's top winter-sports instructors is here. So is a rather dazzling woman, Shirley, from the DSIR; she talks of this and that. Further down the table, Charles Laughton, the playwright and novelist, chats to Josephine and her medium cousin, Mr Mikes. Occasionally one of our lunch guests hoists a video camera to her shoulder; she must be one of the performance collective, Handle With Care. Plus we have the usual assortment of office staff and eager freelances. I have ordered a Sultan's Banquet (twenty-four hours' notice), but with extra Chicken Tikka.

Our business editor, Barry Mendoza, is talking about the new Japanese market in name copyrights. Apparently in the last few years, people with an eye to the future have been registering Western names at the Japanese Chamber of Commerce. Now, for a nominal outlay, one enterprising Tokyo businessman has ended up owning the names of over 2,000 Italian cities and rivers. Refer to Venice in Japan, says Barry, and you pay top rates. In fact, Barry goes on, it makes you wonder about the potential of Maori names; presumably they're just there for the taking. If we don't grab them, some other bugger will.

I glance anxiously at Charles Laughton. How will he react to this sort of talk? But Charles has not heard; his head is inclined towards that of the new Leader of the Opposition, who talks animatedly about the new PVC downpipe and guttering systems.

His nephew has the agency for one of the better systems. It really is the end of rust, you see.

A message. The winter-sports instructor leaves suddenly. A death on the slopes; he must go at once…

Anyway, says Frank, I thought I would start with something on Alexander of Abonitichos and his talking serpent. Then work my way up to the present, with separate entries for people like Le Sieur Themet, favourite of the Empress Josephine; you know, the one who could laugh on one side of his face and cry on the other. And end up with Mr Mikes himself — stressing the local angle, of course, but also the return to the idea of ventriloquism as magic, real old-time belly talking.

But who *is* the ventriloquist in a case like that? I ask. In a way it's really Peter Sellers throwing his voice, isn't it, not Mr Mikes. Assuming the whole thing (I lower my voice) isn't a hoax.

Hoax? says Frank. His mouth drops open. Hoax? You wouldn't know the first thing about it.

Along the table there is talk about the left side of the brain. About the invisible universe. The change of government. The ozone layer. The All Black tour of France.

A man at a nearby table, not one of our party, begins to grow agitated. An odd noise is coming from the floor below him. It is a woman's voice: we can all recognise the faint cries of sexual arousal. The man gets to his knees, lifts the tablecloth. There is nothing there.

The noises grow louder, but now they are coming from another corner of the restaurant. People stop eating; some get to their feet. I watch Frank's lips closely. The voice makes its cries again, small fluttering noises of pleasure and distress. I catch Frank's eye and he smiles, teeth together, lifting his fork in a kind of salute.

Meanwhile our circulation continues to rise, trespassers are prosecuted, life in these islands goes on pressing its case.

Siena

They were travelling in a part of the country famous for its waterfalls. The waterfalls were named after Italian cities, apparently something to do with the new government. They had seen Firenze, a ten-minute walk through bush from a roadside parking lot. A double fan of feathery water: pretty, but nothing special.

It was Jazelle's idea to stop somewhere for a few days. Vicks was sick of driving, so it suited her. And Lucas: who knew what Lucas thought? 'Wherever the road leads on,' he said. He had watched too many old movies. Another tablet fizzed on his tongue.

They had picked him up further down the coast. He had praised the colour of the car and offered himself as a travelling companion. It turned out that he wasn't good company, not in any respect at all really, but neither of the girls had had the heart to tell him. Vicks had come close a couple of times.

Late in the afternoon they found a small hotel. Two storeys, weatherboard, corrugated iron roof. In one direction there was the low whirr of the traffic-way, somewhere out of sight; in the other, a couple of paddocks. Beyond the paddocks the bush started. Off in the distance they could see a glacier, a glint of white.

The hotel toilets said 'Officers' Mess' and 'Powder Room'. On the back of a cubicle door Lucas stared at a rhyme:

Here I sit all broken-hearted,
Paid a penny and only farted.

He repeated it several times at dinner. 'Cheap at the price,' he said, giggling. 'A penny for your thoughts,' he said to the gloomy woman, presumably the publican's wife, who served them. The dining-room had three tables, all set with cutlery, but there were no other guests. The woman brought them shepherd's pie and, to follow, instant pudding with sliced peaches. The hotel had a Fifties emphasis.

The woman had given Vicks and Jazelle a twin room. Blue candlewick bedspreads. They pushed the two beds together. Lucas was by himself in a single along the corridor. You would think that was clear enough.

In one corner of the girls' room a Toogood stood blinking. Its display showed the word 'Burlap'.

'But what was the question?' said Jazelle. To no one in particular.

Lucas put his head around the door. He sidled in and squatted on his haunches. He switched the Toogood to audio.

'Who or what was Phar Lap?' said the Toogood.

Then it said, 'What is a Stevenson screen?'

Then, 'What is the name of the natural home of a beaver?'

'Just as well you don't have a throat,' said Lucas. He flicked open his knife and whispered to himself. His homicidal maniac display. His crazy stuff.

Quack. Vicks farting. *Quack. Quack*. When Vicks farted she made small quacking noises like a duck.

'Straight for the carotid,' said Lucas. 'Every time.' He put a Keepsake on his tongue and grinned as it melted.

Jazelle and Vicks descended to the bar.

Lucas waved his knife at the Toogood.

'What about, "a Canadian dam"?' he said. 'I'll say, "a Canadian dam".'

'Incorrect,' said the Toogood. For some reason it switched itself to hold.

'I'm fifty-seven,' said Lucas, 'too old for this sort of shit.'

The barman was the publican. 'R.P. Heron — Licensed to Sell Spiritous Liquors.' He wore a white shirt and braces. His face looked mildly disappointed above a tartan bow-tie.

'What's your pleasure?' said R.P. Heron.

The room was period décor. Grey lino underfoot, while the bar itself was surfaced in a kind of red formica. The beer came through hoses.

They stayed with the period. Jazelle ordered a Bacardi and Coke.

'Likewise,' said Vicks.

'If you insist,' said Lucas. 'Surprise surprise.'

'Quiet tonight,' said Jazelle.

R.P. Heron explained that the bar was closed except for bona fide guests. And it was mid-week in a slow time of year.

Vicks switched on the holovision. A Nana Mouskouri clone assembled herself.

'Thank you for welcoming me to your home,' she said. 'My music is like a beautiful rainbow. It has no frontiers, no barriers.'

Lucas moved across to the bar. A refill. A double Scotch.

'In my country we try to find a better tomorrow, and tears are mixed with laughter, joy holds hands with sorrow. We sing, dance, and clap hands as all the passions and sorrows come out.'

'That's a decade out,' said Lucas. 'At the very least. If it's the Fifties you have in mind.' He placed a Keepsake on the centre of his tongue.

'I won't be arguing over that one,' said R.P. Heron. He swayed forward on his toes and gave a delicate shrug, like a diver on a high board. 'You do the best you can.'

Nana Mouskouri sang 'The White Rose of Athens'. She swayed as she sang. She walked towards Lucas.

Lucas reached out as if to pull her glasses off, but his hand passed through her head. She made a graceful exit through the wall.

'Steady on son,' said R.P. Heron.

Lucas was the only customer in the bar.

'Our finest hour,' said R.P. Heron. 'Home little bastards home.'

Lucas drifted outside and circumnavigated the hotel. Gravel crunched under his feet. The sky like an instrument panel.

Vicks and Jazelle were in their room. There was a light. Jazelle would be oiling Vicks. Starting with the back of the neck. And then the shoulders.

Upstairs again, he found their door was locked. They had wheeled the Toogood through to his room. It was showing the word 'Mansfield'.

In the morning Jazelle said, 'I do believe it's time Lucas had a taste of the old heave-ho.'

Vicks looked out the window. There was a small jungle gym. A pet lamb was tied to it, and two boys were patting the lamb.

'Whatever you think,' she said. *Quack*.

They went down to look at the lamb. The boys were listening to it. It turned out to be one of the recent implants.

'Legends of the land,' said the taller boy. 'The Sadness of Uenuku. Tawhaki the Bold. The Death of Maui.'

The lamb said, 'After that, each fighting man raised his right hand, in which he was holding his weapon, and held it to his eyes, as though shading them.'

'Rest,' said the smaller boy. Somewhere inside the lamb the voice cut out.

'So what do people do around here?' said Vicks.

'Go to the waterfalls,' said the taller boy.

'Go to the glacier,' said the other. 'Or the waterfalls.'

They aimed vaguely toward the glacier. The road wound up into the hills, sometimes smooth, sometimes bumping through its own potholes. Occasionally they clattered across a one-way bridge. The colour of the water varied, depending on the stream. Milky grey was probably the glacier.

In the back of the car, Lucas chattered on. He had remembered his first visit to the doctor which, now he came to think of it, was his only visit to a doctor. This was still in the days of stethoscopes, if the word meant anything at all.

'So he had this stethoscope thing hanging around his neck, eh, this *listening* device, and he put the ear bits in his ears and the plug end on my chest and listened to my heart beating. "So what can you hear?" I said. He took the plug bit off my chest and pressed it on the top of my head and said, "I hear each one of your very interesting thoughts." Interesting thoughts! My mother thought it was hilarious. I was rigid, absolutely rigid.'

Quack, said Vicks. The road dipped and twisted.

'I was so frightened I didn't know what I was thinking anyway.'

They went slowly uphill. A coach ground past them, hooting. Foreign tourists aimed their lenses. Lucas gave the fingers.

They stopped in a clearing in a beech forest. Lucas stayed in the car.

Someone was selling sandwiches off a trestle table. A girl sold hula hoops. Jazelle looked at them and asked was there only the green colour.

The girl demonstrated.

'When you get to seventy revolutions a minute,' she said, 'you go danger.'

She rotated her body inside the hoop. The hoop went faster and faster, then suddenly spun from green to red.

'Danger,' said the girl. 'As fast as that. Seventy-five dollars.'

They took the walk to the waterfall. Jazelle wore her hoop like a necklace. They looked at the unnaturally thin stream of black water, which descended through several ledges. Its name was Little Napoli. Somewhere there would be a Big Napoli. The water flowed off underground.

They drove to Palermo. There was a giant parking lot. Rows of tents and stalls, amusement parlours, all kinds of vendors.

'Hunger hunger,' said Lucas. Hangi food. Hot dogs. Kebabs. Vegan. He ambled off towards a stall with a large Keepsake sign above it.

Vicks gunned the motor. Vroom vroom.

Jazelle watched through the back window. Lucas had half turned and was watching them go. He held his right hand to his eyes, as though shading them. But the sun was behind clouds.

They drove back slowly. Why hurry? A scenic route looped around the glacier. The road nudged its way through bush, below a jagged ridge of ice.

They stopped at a place for lunch, 'The Diggings', paying for a window view.

'It's in retreat,' said the waiter. He dressed their salads with his back to the glacier. 'They call it negative regime. Come back in 20,000 years.'

Back at the hotel the lamb was asleep. Last rays of afternoon sun.

Vicks tried the hula hoop but couldn't get started. She froze, her knees slightly bent. One of those things.

Jazelle was born for it. She could swing the hoop around her legs, her hips, her waist, her neck. She moved it up and down her body. Then she got up speed. The green slipped to red. But she couldn't hold it steady. The red came and went.

Vicks filmed her. The lamb in the background. Jazelle going in and out of danger.

Vicks and Jazelle sat over their soft drinks. No one else in the bar.

Talking of this and that. Where to go tomorrow.

The holovision was a man in a kilt. He played a piano accordion. The strains of 'Loch Lomond'.

'Surprise surprise,' said Lucas.

He had a Keepsake sway.

Lucas said, 'A double Scotch. And then a double Scotch.'

Vicks and Jazelle concentrated on their lemonade.

'Dinkum?' said R.P. Heron.

The accordion player stopped. He seemed to be out of breath. Mist, a point or two of light, nothing.

'I hitch-hiked down the valley,' said Lucas. 'Old Fifties custom. I got a ride with these Italians.'

He put a Keepsake on his tongue.

'Well, goodnight Mr Heron,' called Vicks.

'You sort of remind me of people I used to know,' said Lucas. 'Mistral. Patchouli. Cumulonimbus. Just say the word.'

Lucas addressed R.P. Heron. 'Tell me,' he said, 'What is the Chandler wobble?'

'Well, I know very little about music as such,' said R.P. Heron.

'This appliance seems a little faulty,' said Lucas. He pointed to his empty glass.

'Steady on,' said R.P. Heron. 'I think you might be getting just a bit shickered. Next thing we'll be having to carry you up to your bed. If you aren't careful.'

'Listen,' said Lucas. 'Listen to me please. I am a real and

historical person, thoroughly researched and well presented. What's the problem?'

Vicks and Jazelle watching from the door.

Lucas with his knife out.

R.P. Heron touched a concealed button with his foot. A bell started ringing.

Lucas slid his knife into R.P. Heron's throat. Easy. R.P. Heron slumped over the bar. There was an oily smell, and a sort of pink liquid oozing from his throat.

Lucas went outside. Sky like an instrument panel. Vicks and Jazelle at their window.

The lamb bleated. Lucas cradled it. He put the point of the knife against its throat.

The lamb said: 'But Papa, the Earth, still loves Rangi, the Sky. And the white mists rise from earth to sky to tell the universe his love, while he weeps for her in the falling dew, and sighs for her in the moaning wind.'

Years later, when they were all in different places, this is how things were.

Whenever Jazelle saw a duck, she remembered Vicks. Quack. And if Vicks saw a circle she might think of a hula hoop, and then she might recall Jazelle. Traffic lights could do it, too: the green and red.

And Lucas: Lucas thought of nothing. There was nothing on his mind.

Vicks and Jazelle never thought of Lucas. The Lucas memories had been over-recorded.

For example, if either of them saw a lamb, or even a picture of a lamb, there came at once to mind the image of a stream of water, falling. The name 'Siena' would float beneath it, like one of those subtitles you used to see in foreign movies. For a minute or two, while it lasted, Vicks and Jazelle would watch the display. Siena was beautiful — milky white and soundless — and it plunged in a single, long, unbroken column for what was apparently a record distance.

The Moon at the End of the Century

That's good then, says Emily to Mr Bliss who shuffles between his two blue suitcases. You'll be in the Neruda Room. It looks out over the water —

Mr Bliss tugs his left ear. I don't want to seem unduly anxious, he says, but I won't *write* like Neruda, will I?

His voice as he asks this question is what I would call an anxious voice.

Not unless you speak Spanish, says Emily. Or think Spanish —

The way Emily talks it's like she leaves a dash at the end of things, hence the dash above. Total abruptness — not dot dot dot, but dash. Emily makes her mind up fast. I got the job here because she liked the fact that I hitch-hiked all the way up from Dunedin, A woman! she said. Alone! Dash!

The thing is, says Emily, you'll write as you are. You have to hear the voice within you — In your case the Bliss voice —

Good good, says Mr Bliss. He just wanted to be sure.

Then Emily tells him about when the evening meal is, about the packed lunch during the day and being free to stroll around etc.

Then she asks Cheryl to show him to his room, and that is what I do, because of course I am Cheryl.

*

Actually I am officially transcription assistant, which means I get up early in the mornings to catch the poems as they come. The poets are timed to wake at half hour intervals, while the poems themselves depend on the circumstances. They are jubilant or sad and all points in between.

Afternoons, I free float but three or four nights a week, depending on how busy Garamond is at the garage, I'm relieving waitress. We never run to more than one main course, but Emily's salads are large and busy and I am authorised to offer a choice of dressings. There's a little notepad next to each place setting, courtesy of the management, for inspiration is known to strike between courses.

Seven would be our limit in busy times but tonight there are three guests only. Emily has put them all at the one table, and I lean in the kitchen doorway by the sweet trolley and enjoy the general awkwardness as Mr Bliss introduces himself.

I'd like it most if you called me Neville, he says.

I scratch my left tit which has been itchy for about three years now, ever since my last time in Nelson as it happens. Outside, somewhere across the paddocks, a siren wails. Wails is the sort of word you can use in prose but not in poetry. It sounds nearby then distant. Even out in the country you can hear the way things happen.

What would that noise be, says Mr Bliss. He has been watching me scratch.

Ambulance or car chase, I say.

Oh, he says, in a voice which manages both pleasure and disappointment, so perhaps it is the Bliss voice. Then he turns back to Lucas, a major dickhead whose main claim to fame is he once got drunk with Sam Hunt, and to Miss Hollywood, her real name, who has been here for three weeks now and is beginning to get some good poems. Or so Emily says.

Mind you, as intelligent people like to say, turrets and dickheads abound in the Nelson district. The other time I was up here, I had just left home. I drifted around craft potteries and psychic healers and ended up scoring a job on a sort of residential therapy farm called Orcadia. Get it? Orcadia? Paradise and killer whales? The clients were women, and they came in because they were feeling a bit down, or a bit out of it, or just disappointed they were women. Mostly they sat in a room among suspended crystals listening to whales singing.

Before the whales and crystals though they each had to have their left breast painted black. True, totally black. It made them fully divisional, whatever that was meant to mean. I knew I was lucky to have a job at all, but I shot through ten seconds after they showed me the cupboard with the cans of paint, it totally freaked me out. I didn't stop till I was back in Oamaru, where Janet Frame grew up, and I've been itching ever since.

Mr Bliss says: Sam Hunt?

Yes, says Lucas. Still full of the old charm charge and chant. But I could tell you a thing or two about rejection slips.

*

I have my clipboard and sit in the wicker chair beside Mr Bliss's bed waiting till he wakes.

Oh Cheryl, he says, there you are.

Some people write stories where the conversations have speechmarks but that's never been my way.

Mr Bliss yawns, then looks anxious, then yawns. The dawn has dawned. His pyjamas are a mustard colour to match his face. I tip my head to one side, like a secretary in films. I try to look encouraging. A pretty girl with a clipboard.

Well…all right…blue, he says, blue for the blue, he says, for the blue of the howl of the churchyard eyes…

Yep, got it.

…and the eyes in pain as they see, now what was it…the love song I think, either the frozen song or the stolen song…

Dot dot dot: for now he drifts and lapses. Now he drifts and lapses…

I'm sorry, he says. His first name is Neville.

But that's miles better than yesterday, I say, using my reassuring voice. Of course, he got nothing yesterday, he hadn't really understood the procedures.

It doesn't sound like me, he says. It's not the sort of thing I usually write.

I sweep back the pale blue curtains so Mr Bliss can look out over the lake. Emily and Garamond refer to 'the lake', but it's basically muddy water screened by clumps of pampas grass. It always looks as if a herd of cows has just gone thundering through. You stand on the bank and look in the water for your face, or even just some clouds, but there's never any reflection.

*

When I came into the world, Oamaru 1977, it was present tense first person. Smack: howl — that's how it felt. Past is past, whatever people say. Present is what's going on, it's inevitable. Future would be best I suppose but as someone says, tomorrow never knows.

Garamond thinks he's inevitable. The truth is, he did grow on me for a while there. It was pretty flattering, past imperfect, but now he's totally finished growing. All this charming stuff, and then the other day he sneaked up behind me in the kitchen and licked the back of my neck. I don't know where Emily was. But I didn't like the way it felt, that oily motor-mechanical tongue. I didn't even like the *idea* of it.

The thing is saving money. How to get enough. How to *amass*. And how to do this poetry job without yawning. How to be nice to all the guests at Goldengrove. How to sidestep Garamond without pissing him off completely. He and Emily take themselves so incredibly seriously. They've both had poems in *Landfall*.

Sydney would be a great place. Cheryl in Sydney — now that would be a bit of. I'd really like to be there for the start of the century, which means I've only got a few months up my sleeve.

But even Wellington would do. I've got to get off the South Island somehow. It's full of missionaries. It slopes downwards. It's so fucking cold at the bottom.

*

Blue for the blue of
the howl of churchyard
eyes, and the eyes
in pain when they see
the stars & all
your stolen lovesongs

The room is quiet. Embarrassed silence. It's as if we all just tiptoed out the door.

You see how much can be done with line-breaks, says Emily.

The rhyme, though, says Lucas. It sounds like it wants to rhyme with blue or eyes or pain. Like, it sort of wants to be something harmonious but it isn't? It doesn't hit the note?

Mr Bliss looks puzzled.

Lucas says: But I'll tell you, Neville, potentially it's my kind of music.

It was just what came into my head, says Neville Bliss.

What were your overnight tapes? says Emily.

Yeats and Elizabethan sonnets. And someone called Jenny Bornholdt.

She comes from Wellington, says Miss Hollywood. I've been on one of her workshops. A handsome woman in her middle years.

Unlike William Butler Yeats, says Lucas.

Mr Bliss looks puzzled. But is that my voice then? he says. Do the linebreaks show it?

We don't know yet, says Emily. We just can't tell — I'll ask Garamond to take a look —

*

Garamond Garamond Garamond.

The name sounds really romantic, like a character in an old book with spiders running up the spine. He's a real cobweb boy. Emily calls him Garamond, the guests call him Garamond, he publishes under the name of Garamond Clarke. But listen to this: his mates at the garage in Richmond call him Gary.

I heard one of them drop him off one night.

See yuh, Gary. Watch out for those poets, haw haw.

Yeah, see yuh, Craig. Thanks, chief. Shuffle shuffle.

He's the local Citroen expert. There's one behind the house and two at the garage. None of them go — he can't get the parts.

I'd say Emily was forty. Garamond would be ten years younger and about twenty years better looking. It's hard to see it lasting.

*

Clipboard time with Neville Bliss. His tapes last night were Dylan Thomas and James K. Baxter. Lethal stuff. He drones on and on, I've covered five sheets of paper already.

The moon, he says, makes havoc of the stars, each time I glimpse you in between the passing cars. In the macrocarpa shade you sing because you are. No wait a minute: yes, because you are. Like a rat without zips, you are happy.

Silence. Mr Bliss sits back. He says: That's it. It's really coming now, isn't it?

Do you mean a rat without *zip*, Mr Bliss? Without get-up-and-go? Or is it plural rats?

No, says Neville Bliss. A rat without zips.

Well, it's a bit private.

Maybe I have a private voice, he says. Maybe that's what I'm beginning to learn thanks to all you good people. Then he tells me a long story about how he took early retirement and then his house filled up with rats.

They had zips on them, you see, Cheryl. Or at least I thought they had zips on them. I put food down for them, lots of saucers. I made holes in the floor so they could come and go.

But that's disgusting. Didn't they teach you hygiene at school? The great plague and stuff?

Ah but the rats had zips — this was the worrying thing. I was scared that if something happened, or if I reported them, the authorities would come and undo the zips.

So? Why would that be so bad?

Because, Cheryl, then all the human beings would have come out.

*

Poetry is funny stuff all right. At Sunnyside thcy used it to make Neville Bliss a bit less mad, and here he is at Goldengrove, a half-way happy fellow, struggling away with the Bliss voice. But the hired help, the whole one of me, is going slowly up the wall because of poetry. Today for example —

The thunder says you have no choice,
my cold blues baby
with your blue Antarctic voice…

Lucas looks pleased with himself. You can see he really thinks he's hit the music.

Miss Hollywood tips forward in her chair. She has black eyes and for a moment she narrows them.

It just strikes me as very strange, says Miss Hollywood, that when I use the phrase Antarctic lace in a poem very generally admired, and which I have been advised — she looks sideways at Emily — to offer to *Landfall*, it simply strikes me as rather strange that a few days later I encounter the phrase Antarctic voice in something written by a fellow guest and student.

You can't copyright Antarctica, says Lucas. It's a natural feature, Antarctica's *there*. Right, Cheryl?

Don't bring me in, I say. I'm just here to keep an accurate record.

I wave my ballpoint in the interests of accuracy.

I can see what Alice means, though, says Neville. On the other hand, can anyone actually own a word? I spent some time yesterday thinking about this one, and as I understand it…

*

What decides me is when Garamond makes another pass.

We are in the kitchen. I am scratching, as I think discreetly, when he says, Here let me help you with that, Cheryl, and grabs a handful. I knee him in the place they teach you to at school.

He drops to the floor and goes: Ug ug ug ug ug, and I drop the pohutukawa teatowel on him.

Mess with Cheryl at your peril, I say. There's a wee poem for you, Gary.

*

Emily comes to see me in the morning.

I'm sorry, Cheryl, she says. He's a poet, that's what it is. And young — You know how poets are —

Then it all gets very businesslike. Two weeks pay in lieu of, dash. Shuttlefare to Wellington, all right dash. Farewell drinks tomorrow, no hard feelings —

*

So it is that we are all down by the muddy water, late afternoon, well into our amicable session with a few bottles of Winegut.

Garamond is keeping clear of the hired help but is very jolly, none the worse for wear. Did you hear, he says, they've found the tenth planet? Planet X. It was on television the other night, it's way out past Pluto.

Imagine, says Emily.

Are you sure ten? says Lucas. That's more than I remember.

I make a contribution. Mercury, I say. Venus, Earth, Mars, Jupiter, Saturn, Uranus, Neptune, Pluto.

Plus Janus, says Garamond.

Janus? says Lucas.

That's what they're calling it, says Garamond. The new planet.

Christ, says Lucas, who chooses these names?

They're gods, says Miss Hollywood. The universe is filled with gods. Janus is the god of doorways and new beginnings. Janus is the two-faced god who looks both ways.

She says this as if she's reciting.

You missed something out, Cheryl, says Neville Bliss. He looks pleased and somehow surreptitious.

What's that?

Well, where do you put the moon in all that?

The moon isn't a planet, I say. Moons go round planets. There are more moons than the one up there.

Mr Bliss looks blank, it's called alliteration. How do you mean? he says.

Look, I say, there's elementary stuff that some of you people just don't seem to know. It shows in your poems all the time — like the way you say the moon *shines*.

Well it does, says Miss Hollywood. She points to the far edge of sky where the pale three-quarters disc is visible.

But it doesn't, it *reflects*. The moon reflects the light from the sun. What you can see up there is the moon's daylight.

So what I call moonlight, you'd call sunlight? says Lucas. Do me a favour, Cheryl.

Neville Bliss has fallen silent. He has that anxious look again.

Emily and Garamond are drifting up towards the house, mildly tipsy, holding hands...

You're being very *literal*, Cheryl, says Miss Hollywood.

*

Now if this were the real thing — torture territory, genuine red-hot Oamaru Gothic — round about now would be the place for the big shock that of course you've been expecting.

And here comes Emily right on time, screaming down from the house waving the metal carving knife — and coming straight at me, you'll be pleased to know. Mr Bliss whimpers. Or hang on, is it Garamond, it's hard to tell at this distance, all you can really take in are the hands covered in blood...But no, it's Emily, here she comes, walking very slowly now, naked to her middle-aged waist. Oh my god! Her left breast is painted black…

Ha! ha! ha! she goes. Ha! ha! ha!

Joke.

This is just a story about things at the end of the century, which wasn't as we all know the end of the world, and I want to end with the last thing I saw.

*

I decided to show the poets how the solar system worked. Then you'll know about outer space as well as inner space, I said.

Mr Bliss, I said, come over here, and just stand still. You're a star called Sol. You just stand here and shine. You can lift your arms if you like.

Good, I said, you do that beautifully.

Then I asked Miss Hollywood to walk round him in a wide circle.

So I'm Earth, she said, because she understood.

Now it's time for the moon, I said, and I got Miss H to go just a little bit more slowly so that Lucas, holding his glass of Chablis, could circle round her without some terrible collision.

This is hard work, said Lucas. What happens if the moon trips over?

You spill your wine, said Miss Hollywood.

That's how we learnt it at school, I said, Oamaru South 1983, Miss Fahey's room. Just for a moment I glimpsed my mum, somewhere in the back of my head, waiting for her weekly package from the Rosicrucians…

Round and round they went. They were enjoying themselves.

Moon is still a pretty word, said Miss Hollywood.

Sure is, said Lucas. I wouldn't be without it.

Mr Bliss stood still and watched the sky. He held his arms out and the others moved around him. It's freely available, he said. That's the thing I like.

I walked back towards the house a step at a time, going slowly backwards. It was early evening, about a month before the end of the century. The moon shone in the sky and I wondered what it would be like to be weightless. It was a month before the end of the century and I watched the poets shine and circle, discussing the language fit for verse.

The Days of Sail

There is a photograph of early Dunedin, taken from the top of the Town Hall in 1883. It shows the lower side of the Octagon: the mouth of Lower Stuart Street to the left, of Princes Street to the right. In the middle distance, and probably the photographer's subject, First Church stands on its hillock. Beyond it you can make out reclaimed land and warehousing. Further off the masts of ships lift above the harbour.

The photograph was taken by John R. Morris. You can find it in a book of early Dunedin photographs from the Hardwicke Knight collection. 'People and vehicles,' says an accompanying note, 'have moved during the time exposure so that the streets appear empty.'

And it is true: the small town is like a child's model. Spires and shopfronts; a Sunday morning silence; a place which will never have a human population. It is possible to guess where people may have been: that faint blur, there, on the pavement; those marks that look like brush-strokes on the surface of the road. In fact, if you gaze carefully — as I am gazing now — you will see that one or two human figures have persisted. A tiny man stands outside Smith and Smith, next to a horse. On the corner of Princes Street and the Octagon another man stands in front of W. Absolon Smith, Tailor. He wears a dark suit and hat, and is staring intently towards the centre of the Octagon. He looks as if he is watching a procession, or waiting at a set of traffic lights. But of course in the Dunedin of 1883 there is no such thing as a set of traffic lights.

The lower half of the photograph is history. But the upper half is sky: a uniform white, a white wholly without blemish, intruded upon only by the slender, ascending spire of First Church. It is tempting to imagine that the photographer stared out from the top of Dunedin Town Hall at a cloudless nineteenth-century blue: cerulean. But there must have been clouds. They would have been moving too fast for the camera to take them in.

The Queen looks down from her high window above Princes Street. What a dump, she thinks. What a ghastly hole.

The empty streets.

Some man is telling her that Dunedin means 'Eden on the hill'. He is explaining that she is visiting a city of firsts.

The skirl of the pipes. A highland band goes by. *Snap*. The Queen takes a photograph. *Ho-ro you nutbrown maiden.*

Yes, says the civic dignitary, who stands slightly behind his monarch, speaking over her shoulder, we can for example lay claim to the nation's first university, the University of Otago, founded 1869.

A haka party goes by on the deck of a lorry. *Snap*.

We can also boast the first secondary school for girls, indeed the first in the Empire, 1870.

Commonwealth, says the Queen. She waves.

The empty streets. A brass band goes by. *Snap*.

The first woollen mills, 1874. The first daily newspaper, 1861. The first shipment of frozen meat home to the old country, aboard a ship named for our city, the *Dunedin*, 1882.

Marching girls. *Snap*. A band of assassins. *Snap*.

Why, says the civic dignitary, the list is endless.

I am told, remarks the Queen, that on its first voyage the *Dunedin* carried in all the carcasses of some 4,908 sheep and lambs.

I believe so, ma'am.

(The Queen is always extensively briefed on these visits.)

And that after nine further voyages the *Dunedin* was lost without trace in the year 1890, perhaps, some believe, having struck an iceberg off the Cape of Good Hope. And that she and all her complement and cargo now rest in a watery grave.

I believe so, ma'am. Also the first kindergarten, St Andrew's Hall, 1889.

A line of lorries goes by. Local actors are dressed to represent the first professors of the University.

The Professor of Classics. *Snap*. The Professor of Mathematics, at a blackboard. *Snap*. The Professor of Mental Science. *Snap*. The Professor of English Language and Literature. *Snap*. The Professor of Natural Philosophy. *Snap*. Chemistry. *Snap*. Biology. *Snap*. Mining and Mineralogy. *Snap*. Anatomy and Physiology...

But the Queen has run out of film.

Ours too was the first School of Medicine in the land, says the civic dignitary. To us it fell also to appoint the first woman professor in New Zealand, Professor W.L. Boys-Smith, head of the faculty of Home Science.

But the Queen has run out of small talk.

She turns from the window and addresses one of her security men.

Tell me, she says, what has four legs and goes 'tick-tock'?

Ma'am?

A watchdog, says the Queen.

It could be anyone at all in that 1883 photograph, standing outside a tailor's shop on the corner of Princes Street and the Octagon, just across from the spot where the Star Fountain once played music in the evenings. As it happens, I believe the man may be my great-grandfather, Priam Murphy, after whom I am named. A sense of remoteness makes him look older than the thirty-three years he would have been then.

In the photograph you can see that small trees and shrubs have been recently planted in the Octagon. I am also certain it is these trees at which my great-grandfather is staring so intently. Each is encircled by a fence, about waist-high. Not much can be done about the wind, but at least the young trees can be protected from the depradations of browsing wagon-horses and wandering stock. Strange to say, the greatest danger comes from boys playing football. They do not care where they run, or on what they trample. There are no flowerbeds in the Octagon in 1883, and for good reason.

My great-grandfather is keeping an eye on the trees and shrubs. After all, he had a hand in planting them. It is a thankless task. Most passers-by find him amusing. Yet he will have his reward, although he does not know this yet.

Just at the moment, however, he cannot see the boys chasing after the flying ball. He cannot see the horse which suddenly panics when it is struck by a ball outside Smith and Smith. Everything is moving too fast to leave any impression.

In Great King Street, not far from the Captain Cook Hotel, there are several buildings which belong to the university's School of Medicine. The building with which I am associated has an official name and street number, but most people know it as 'The Sheep-Dip'. Few could tell you why. Most would say it was one of those funny, local names. Perhaps in early days settlers had a sheep-dip there...

The Sheep-Dip is seven storeys high. It has as many floors as Dunedin's — and New Zealand's — first skyscraper, the Mutual Funds Building, erected in 1910.

My name is Priam Murphy, and each day I make my way to the seventh floor of the Sheep-Dip to see to the current residents.

The room is large, rectangular. One wall boasts a portrait of the Queen, red-jacketed and side-saddle, on her horse Burmese. If, like John R. Morris a hundred years ago, I want to look out across the city, I must clamber over the double aluminium farm gates which cut the room in two, edge my way past half a dozen drowsy sheep and stare out through a small window. Then there is a view of the far side of the harbour. Grey of water, green of hills, cloudy blue of sky. In front and to the right are hospital buildings. If I crane my neck a little, I can see to the left the Museum Reserve and the main entrance to the museum itself.

Each day I sweep and shovel shit away. Sheep have tidy droppings, so it is not a particularly messy business. I set down food — artificial mixtures, some of it in granule form, some of it a rough mash pudding which I make up myself from a base of pulped swede turnip. I examine scars and check for newcomers.

I look to see who might be missing. How is Princess Anne today? And where is the Queen Mother?

I look under the straw, too, to see if anyone has tampered with the gun.

My name is Priam Murphy. I am a member of the university ground staff. The sheep blink at me, their eyes full of dark reproach. As if I were the one who insisted on all this! As if I myself might raise the knife above them!

Yet they are right, I am culpable, I accept things as they are. My aunt does not. She says that I am her beautiful boy but I am one of those songs in which the melody gives advice to the words. I sing the song of circumstance, I do as the tune tells me.

Here is a true story which my aunt told me.

Not so long ago, a seventeen-year-old, Marcus Serjeant, was sent to prison for five years for firing a gun with intent to alarm the Queen. On Saturday 13 June 1981 the Queen was riding down the Mall for the annual ceremony of Trooping the Colour. Six pistol shots rang out. The Queen was courage itself; she kept control of her horse Burmese, which almost bolted.

Serjeant's gun contained blanks, and he was quickly subdued by angry members of the public. For a while his life was in considerable danger.

Serjeant had written to the Queen, warning her to stay at home on 13 June. 'There is an assassin out to get you.'

He described himself clearly. But no one saw him coming.

My great-grandfather, the first Priam Murphy, came to Dunedin from Melbourne in 1877. Like most others he was too late for the gold, but he knew a thing or two about seeds and plants, so hired himself out as a gardener and set up in business in a quiet way importing seeds and plants from England. By the mid-1880s he had his own retail outlet in George Street and a fairly large nursery in North East Valley. There are four bungalows on the old nursery site now. I live in one of them with my aunt. It is my house. I have taken her in. In some ways, I suppose, she has taken me in.

Remember Tangiwai, my aunt says.

It wasn't long before Priam Murphy had become an informal consultant to the city fathers, and one of the prime movers in the newly founded Amenities Society. It was the Amenities Society which successfully campaigned to have Dunedin's public reserves planted and properly tended. Many felt that the Octagon especially had become a mark of reproach, a blotch on a city whose whole originating impulse had been a vision of moral beauty. My great-grandfather worked in closely with the local councillors. It was he who decided on the Oriental plane trees for the Octagon, and the trees themselves — like those in Queens Gardens and the Museum Reserve — came through the North East Valley nursery. When the council brought David Tannock out from Kew Gardens as Superintendent of Parks and Reserves, Priam Murphy felt he had done his work. He watched from a distance as Tannock created the Botanical Gardens. He never voiced disapproval but there was something pointed about the speed with which he offered his services to the university, supervising two full-time groundsmen for only a small honorarium.

My great-grandfather was a man of ideas before he was a man of substance. It was he who dreamed up the first large shipment of hedgehogs in 1885. His scheme was mocked in the newspaper, but he was convinced the hedgehog would quickly adapt and come to control a wide range of garden pests. Time has proved him right. My aunt says that if she could have sixpence for every hedgehog in Dunedin, she would have enough money to move to Auckland.

My aunt is a frail, nondescript woman. In the street you would probably fail to notice her coming towards you. She has no more substance than a reflection in the window of Arthur Barnetts — a thin grey figure flitting through the new display of winter coats.

She loves jigsaws. She has just finished 'The Death of Captain Cook' and is making a start on a new one. At the moment she is sitting quite still, gazing at the image on the box. A tiny, two-masted ship is perched on the horizon near the middle of the painting. It is caught between a furious blue ocean and a sky of wild, unsteady grey. The ship seems the least important thing on view, though it attracts the eye.

The painter has called his picture 'The Days of Sail'. There are 1,800 pieces.

The Queen visits Dunedin from time to time, although not as often as many citizens would like. In 1954 Leonard Wright got a knighthood out of it. But she made no sign of coming here on her latest New Zealand trip — something which many locals took as a personal slight, while others saw in it confirmation of the city's slow decline. The Queen preferred a swamp near Wellington. She stood on her wooden platform and saw, instead of swamp-birds, the white helmets of crouching policemen.

But the Queen was in Dunedin on the afternoon of 14 October 1981, just a few months after the episode with Marcus Serjeant. Mid-October is a difficult time of year in Dunedin. Too late, certainly, for the rhododendrons at the Botanical Gardens, but a little early for the azaleas. Hence the decision to visit the Science Fair at the museum in Great King Street, just across the road from the Sheep-Dip.

My aunt is my mother's sister. Both girls were born in Auckland and came down here to study medicine. My mother fell in love with one of the university gardeners and for her that was the end of that. My aunt found she could not bear the separation from her sister, so came and lived with us, helping my mother keep house. I have a photograph of the family at St Clair. I am holding my aunt's hand. We are standing beside my mother who is buried up to her neck in the sand. We look pleased with ourselves, as if between us we have just invented the whole idea of a day at the beach. My father must have taken the photograph since he is nowhere to be seen.

My aunt does her jigsaws and likes the occasional sherry.

On becoming soldiers, she says, we do not cease to be citizens.

She sorts the pieces of her new jigsaw puzzle into two separate piles: one of cloud, one of water.

My aunt calls me her beautiful boy but I am nearly fifty. I have a ginger beard, a barrel chest and am already quite bald. I do as the tune tells me, though I am far from musical. People tell me I look like a pirate. But I do not have a parrot on my shoulder.

I am an employee of the University of Otago, a minor member of the ground staff. Both my father and my grandfather were Head Gardener, a position first created after the death of Priam Murphy. But I have not risen to such heights. I know nothing of plants and trees. I can tell a pine tree from a rose bush, but finer discriminations are beyond me. Through me the university maintains a family tradition; it also shows sympathy in the matter of my father's death.

I do very ordinary jobs. I mow the lawns below the Clock Tower. I move compost to and fro in a wheelbarrow and throw weeds on the incinerator. Each day I go to the seventh floor of the Sheep-Dip. The half-dozen sheep, crossbred ewes and wethers, stare at me with dark, reproachful eyes. They think I am going to choose one of them for surgery. But it is tomorrow that Princess Anne will have her hysterectomy. It is tomorrow that Lord Snowdon will receive the kidney which was yesterday removed from Princess Michael.

It is not my job to get the country's medical students off to a good start in the world of surgery. That is not how I think of myself. No, I am here to pulp the swede turnip and remove the sheep droppings. I am here to worry about the gun, to wonder what it is for, and why no one else has seen it.

14 October 1981

The Queen and Prince Philip have flown to Dunedin. They drop out of the sky on a lightning visit. Within half an hour of their noon arrival they are in the midst of one of their habitual walkabouts, strolling informally in the Octagon, chatting to the Mayor about the agreeable spring weather, and admiring the plane trees which are just coming into leaf.

It is a time of special offerings. The Queen accepts posies and bouquets as they come to her, until her arms are full of flowers. One lady displays a tea-towel with a border of tiny Union Jacks. Another shows the Queen a large photograph of the Royal Family in July 1947, taken at the time of the Queen's engagement to Prince Philip. A small girl shows a picture of her kitten.

But there are discordant notes. Toward the end of the walkabout there are representatives of the usual protest groups. Maori radicals. IRA sympathisers. Republicans. The unemployed. Lesbians. There are placards and banners. 'The Empire Is Dead'. 'Go Home Irihapeti'. Some of the demonstrators are chanting: 'Jobs not tours! Jobs not tours!' Loyal onlookers set up a rival cry: 'We love the Queen! We love the Queen!'

But the Queen does not hear. She has already been whisked off to lunch at the Southern Cross Hotel.

I have a cutting from the next morning's *Otago Daily Times*, which shows my aunt holding a photograph up before the Queen. The caption underneath reads *Yes, that's me!* The Queen is pointing and smiling, her arms are full of flowers.

I asked my aunt about this quite recently, and she said she felt she had to be absolutely sure.

Christmas Eve 1953. 10.21 p.m.

The Wellington-Auckland express plunges through a bridge into the suddenly swollen Whangaehu River, about a mile north of Tangiwai. There are 285 passengers aboard the train but only 134 survive.

My mother and father were planning to visit my mother's parents in Auckland. They had packed Christmas presents. They also hoped they might see the Queen there. They said they would tell her to look out for me when she got to Dunedin. They thought this was a great joke.

It is not clear why they set off to the North Island without taking me. I was fourteen. It was Christmas, a special time of year. Perhaps I didn't want to go. My aunt says that my mother said on the station platform that she needed a little fillip and my father said Elizabeth already had him.

It was confusing at the time and that is how it goes on. Everything runs together, caught up in the unimaginable mass of water which bore off bridge and carriages and stripped many victims of their clothes and shoes.

My parents left me a bicycle for Christmas. My mother's body was returned to Dunedin for burial. I never saw her. My father was never found. His was one of twenty bodies which were never accounted for. My aunt says he was probably swept out to sea. Even the train's carriages ended up several miles downstream. Shoes were being washed up on the beaches around Wanganui throughout 1954.

I ran up the stairs of the Sheep-Dip. I was probably too late, but all the same I ran.

The sheep were huddled in a corner, a chorus of worried bleats proceeding from expressionless faces. Beneath the window Princess Margaret lay unmoving on the straw. Her skull had been crushed, blood leaked from it.

I knelt beside her. All I could guess was a heavy blow.

A heavy blow all right. But where was the gun?

The Queen's car draws up outside the Otago Museum. The civic luncheon at the Southern Cross has gone off rather well. Now it is time to inspect the New Zealand Science Fair with its experimental exhibits showing research and technical skills in the fields of biological and physical sciences, and applied science and technology. Now it is time for the Queen to walk beneath trees planted by my great-grandfather a hundred years ago.

Suddenly there is a loud report — like a firecracker, or a rifle shot. The Queen's police officer, Commander Trestrail, looks worried. Men around the royal car begin to reach into their inside jacket pockets.

But there is no need to panic. The Queen has heard nothing. It may only have been a metal traffic sign being knocked over. It may only have been a vehicle backfiring. The Queen steps from her car on to the footpath.

And the museum visit goes ahead without delay. The Queen is

particularly tickled by a device entitled 'Mouse Power', showing mice running almost perpetually on a wheel to produce energy. On a more serious note, the Duke learns that the regional science fairs — there are now thirteen of them — usually involve as many as 5,000 exhibitors, young and old, every year.

In all it is a brief but highly successful visit. Perhaps the only discordant note comes from the Queen's outfit. The pale blue coat and hat she wears in Dunedin have already been seen before. During a visit to the Elphin Showground in the City Park at Launceston, Tasmania, only eight days earlier, she wore exactly the same outfit.

My aunt has filled the sky with cloud. Now she is deciding on the first pieces of blue.

One of the sheep butted me, she says. Just as I was taking aim. I ended up pulling the trigger far too soon. I just swung around and hit it in the head. It wasn't part of any grand design.

You had better give me the gun, I say. We'll have to get rid of it.

What gun? says my aunt. You're a dear boy, Priam, but I haven't the faintest idea what you're talking about.

I explain to the others in the creative writing workshop that my great-grandfather simply pushed his way into the story.

'I didn't mean him to play much part at all. He just got bigger and bigger.'

'I wonder if you could use him somewhere else,' says Tom. 'See, perhaps you've really got several stories here.'

Jane says that, as a character, she likes the great-grandfather more than the aunt.

'Are they both true, or did you make them up?'

I explain that my great-grandfather is based on historical fact but that the aunt is pretty much my own invention.

'I *thought* so,' says Jane.

'You meet people like that, though,' says Allen. 'She's not unlike any number of aunts really.'

'What about this Sheep-Dip idea?' says Tom. 'I had friends at

Med. School and I've never heard that name. Not that I want to make realism a test of everything.'

'Oh it is,' says Sally. 'Is the name for the building I mean. I thought you read it out beautifully.'

'I made up the names for the sheep,' I say. 'They just came to me as a sort of silly idea.'

'Well it's really very striking for a first attempt,' says Fiona. 'I think you have every right to feel encouraged, Tony. The first section's almost a story in itself. That's where the most accomplished *writing* is.'

'My point exactly,' says Tom. 'It's really more than one story.'

'Well,' says Fiona. 'I think the main thing is that you *do* something with it. Send it off somewhere.'

My name is Anthony Priam Murphy. I mow the lawns below the Clock Tower and look after the university sheep. My aunt and I live together in a house in North East Valley. In the evenings she works at her jigsaw puzzles, while I puzzle over my short stories.

My aunt says I am her beautiful boy but that I am like the hedgehog who curls up in the middle of the road when traffic is approaching. She talks to me about my poor emotional posture. She puts a book on her head and walks up and down in my bedroom to show what she means.

She tucks me up and turns out the light. She says, 'Sweet dreams.'

But she does not believe in dreams.

In our creative writing workshop we have started keeping dream notebooks. We keep an exercise book by the bed; and when we wake, we write down everything we can remember. Then we try to make something out of it.

In tonight's dream my father and grandfather and great-grandfather are standing on the deck of a ship which has just docked at Port Chalmers. They look down towards me but they do not move towards the gangplank.

They know they are too late for the gold.

'Come ashore!' I call to them. 'Come ashore!'

They make no response. But surely they can hear me…

I begin to sing a song of welcome. The melody is beautiful. I do not understand the words but know that they are part of the beauty.

All the time that I am singing I stand absolutely still. My great-grandfather, the first Priam Murphy, dissolves. Of course. My grandfather dissolves, too.

My father hesitates, then moves towards the gangway…

This is a dream. At any moment I may wake. Clouds pour across the sky and my lungs fill with air as though they might be sails.

Flights of Angels

Clinton threw his schoolbag through the door and raced in after it. Then he drew himself up to look tall, a thing he's been anxious about lately, and told me.

'*Hamlet*?' I said. 'Rosebank Normal doing a production of *Hamlet*? But you're all little kids.'

'Well, we are,' said Clinton, who is my only son, my only *child*, who is also only ten years old. 'Doing it, I mean. And guess what?' he said.

'What?'

'I'm it.'

'What do you mean, *it*?'

'Hamlet. I'm Hamlet.'

'I don't believe you,' I said. 'This is stupid. Go and hang up your bag.'

'No,' said Clinton, 'It's true. I'm the prince of Denmark, it's the leading role.'

'I know what the leading role in *Hamlet* is,' I said. 'I know all about the eponymous hero. The bit I don't believe is you. You're only ten,' I said. 'Or have you forgotten?'

Clinton started talking to me slowly, a bit like Brendan used to. 'Miss Kitteredge is all in favour, and Mr Speight agrees. I did an audition. I was pretty good. Oh what a rogue and pleasant slave am I.'

'*Peasant* slave,' I said.

'Yeah, something like that. Take it easy, Mum.'

I talked to Brendan. Every Saturday when he drops Clinton back, he comes in for a cup of tea. We slide a few words back and forth across the kitchen table. One time last month he even stayed for fish-and-chips. But I think by the time we were munching the last cold chips, I knew we wouldn't be getting back together. He didn't even stay for the Lotto results.

'So, what do you want me to do, Carol?'

'I don't want you to do anything. You're his father, you're actually involved in this, strange as it may seem to you. You can't just take him to a movie and then forget it all till the next time.'

'Want to know what movie?'

'No.'

'It was *Hamlet*. The new Mel Gibson one.'

'Shit, Brendan, whose side are you on?'

'Look, Carol, there are kids his age playing the piano in Tokyo concert halls: genius musicians. Anyway, why shouldn't he be in *Hamlet* if he wants to? Remember Stalin. You could think of it as an honour, if you wanted. Is this stuff Earl Grey? It doesn't taste quite right to me.'

'All those lines,' I said. 'And what about the sword fights? What if he gets hurt?'

Brendan leant across the table and ran his finger round the lid of the teapot. Then he lifted the lid and peered in. 'Tea-bags,' he said. 'I could tell. Look, the only thing that upsets me is that I'll be probably be out of the country. I won't even get to see him.'

'Not Tokyo?'

'Yeah, sure thing Carol, Tokyo. Why not.'

Brendan is a sort of aspiring jazz drummer. He's been aspiring for about ten years now. Every so often he heads off to Tokyo for classes with this jazz-drumming expert who — so he once told me — could pass for a Japanese cousin of Orson Welles. Brendan even has a set of practice drums he got over there. They make no noise — you can fold them up and store them away under the bed. Maybe if he'd got them a bit earlier... Or maybe not. I think the silence probably suits him: he hates it when happiness is loud.

'That's hopeless, Brendan. You can't just clear off when your son's got the lead part in William Shakespeare's *Hamlet*. The *title* role. You're his father, for Heaven's sake.'

Clinton came into the room at that moment, or maybe just before. He put his hands on his hips and stared at Brendan. 'Bloody, bawdy villain!' he said. 'Remorseless, treacherous, lecherous, kindless villain!'

'Kindless?' I said, after Brendan had shuffled out the door.

'That's what the text says, Mum. Kindless means unnatural.'

Clinton is a gifted child. It can all get a bit tiresome sometimes.

I didn't make a proper appointment to see Gerry Speight, but I brought it up at Wednesday-night table tennis.

'Five love, service, love five — come on, Carol, concentrate,' he said. He faced me over the net, shifting from foot to foot, his orange sweater as wide as the table.

I said: 'Gerry, he's ten years old, you don't even let him do Woodwork.'

'As for Woodwork, I've never been approached,' said Gerry Speight. 'But you know what a privilege I think it is to have a boy like Clinton at Rosebank. As headmaster, I'm on the side of mainstreaming, of course; but I agree with Judy Kitteredge, you have to go on finding the right sort of challenges.'

'Look, apart from the fact that *Hamlet* is a totally deranged idea in the first place, all the other kids in the cast will be a lot older.'

'Most of them, most of them.'

'He'll be totally out of his depth. Why can't you do something nice by Margaret Mahy? Some librarians and pirates.'

'Love six. He shone in the audition — really shone — none of the bigger kids could touch him. And Judy's producing the play — you know how sensible she is.'

'Do I?'

'Yes, you do. Plus remember there are senior members of the teaching staff in major roles.'

'Yes,' I said. 'I heard about that — Mr Tucker as the grave-digger.'

'And I'm involved too, Carol. Judy's cast me as the ghost. I finish early, I can keep an eye on things.'

'And the sword fights?'

'Look, Carol, you can forbid him to take part. You can write me a formal note if that's what you want. A formal note to that effect. But remember this is an extraordinarily gifted child we're talking about. Remember his Stalin project?'

I rang Brendan.

'You can't go, Bren — not to Tokyo, I mean. You encouraged him, not me. I can't cope with this stuff on my own. I mean, you never had to live with Stalin.'

'It was just a school project — graphs and pictures.'

'My God, all those pages. All those purges. It was the Kirov assassination finished me off.'

'I'm not going, anyway, Carol. We've had a talk. I'm going to hear Clinton's lines.'

'*You*? I'm the one with a BA in English.' I suddenly remembered walking across the town hall stage to get it: black italic handwriting, and the big red seal of Otago University. Where had it gone?

'He feels you're unsympathetic — quite rightly in my opinion. Your only problem is you'll have to let me visit in the evenings. See, you were right, what you said the other day. He's my son, I'm going to get him through this thing.'

I listened to them practise through the wall. Brendan was Gertrude, Claudius, Ophelia, Polonius — one by one and sometimes, it felt like, all at once. But all the inhabitants of Elsinore sounded like Brendan — a sort of dismal monologue somewhere beyond the gib-board. I could never quite pick up Clinton's voice, but sometimes there was the sound of two hands clapping — Brendan applauding our son's soliloquies.

One night after Brendan had gone, Clinton came through and asked me to tell him how he got his name.

'I know you've told me, but I like to hear.'

'Have you brushed your teeth and stuff? Okay, then hop in the bed.'

I told him how he was born in Brendan's panel van just outside of Clinton. It was a dark, wet night. We were heading for the hospital when the van broke down.

'You weren't actually born in the van, you were *nearly* born in it. The ambulance got to us in time and took us through to Gore.'

'Was Dad pleased?'

'About the van?'

'No, was he pleased when I was born?'

I looked at my ten-year-old, gifted son — brown eyes, black hair — who lay in the bed beside me. I remembered Brendan sitting in the back of the ambulance, a funny, tender look in his eyes, panting his way through my contractions.

'He was really pleased. Fathers generally are.'

'Mum?'

'Mmm.'

'Did Dad ever pop the big question?'

Something fluttered in my throat. 'What big question? To be or not to be?'

'No, you know, the *question*.'

'Oh, *that* question. Why don't you ask him?'

'I did.'

'And what did he say?'

'He says he thinks he probably did but he can't remember.'

'Well,' I said, 'as a matter of fact, he did, and I said no.'

'Why? Why did you say no?'

I tried to remember. Did we even use words? Suddenly I remembered where my BA degree was — rolled up in the suitcase under the bed.

'Oh, I don't know, Clinny. He was too casual or something.'

'Did he kneel?'

'He did actually. Yes he actually did kneel, he went right down on his knees. It's just he was seven months too late.'

A couple of nights later, Brendan turned up with the video of Olivier's *Hamlet*. He settled on the sofa and sent out for pizzas.

I could remember seeing it at school: mist and darkness, dizzying ramparts. We watched the camera float around the castle corridors. Someone came to the door with pizzas and we paused.

'I hate all the dissolves, don't you?' said Brendan.

'He's too blonde,' I said. 'Olivier.'

'And he looks too old,' said Clinton.

'Good, though,' said Brendan, 'this Hawaiian Special.'

The two of them spent the rest of the night saying the words along with the actors, especially the voice-overs.

As the credits rolled across, Brendan said: 'It's usually romance or money, but my horoscope this morning said that I should prepare to have a semi-mystical conversation in the near future.'

'Well,' I said. 'This particular household never gets very transcendental.'

'Too bad,' he said. It sounded like an exit line, and after it he left.

'So how's it going?' I said to Clinton later. 'I know you know your lines.'

'It's going good, really good.'

'Going well. Even Shakespeare didn't talk like that.'

'Whatever. Mr Speight's mother died, so he's been away a bit. But he told us she was ready to go. He hasn't hidden it or anything. Miss Kitteredge says that anyway you need to be open to your emotions if you're doing Shakespeare. We've decided that I won't really be mad, I'll just feign madness.'

'Good,' I said, 'I'm pleased about that.' Then I said: 'The impossibility of fixity in a world of flux.'

'What's that, Mum?'

'It was an essay topic we had: support, refute or modify. I think I supported, with some modification.'

'That's a bit intellectual for me, Mum. Now, Mum, can I get you anything? Would you like a Milo, or a glass of wine?'

'Well, this is a change. What's come over you?'

'Dad says I've got to be more of a help to you.'

'Does he? When did he say that, Clinton?'

'Oh, he says it all the time. He's always saying stuff like that.'

It would have been rude not to, somehow, so I actually went with Brendan, but I made a point of paying for my own seat. The programme had a discreet note: 'This production is dedicated to the memory of Edith Speight. Goodnight, sweet lady.' It made me want to cry — or laugh — so I stared straight ahead for a couple of minutes while Brendan wriggled in his seat.

The play was silly and brilliant, the way Shakespeare is, with the comic bits and sad bits all getting along extremely well together, as they're supposed to. 'A collage of styles, lyrical, grotesque and grand,' is what I remember our lecturer saying, and I remember how he paused for a while, wiping his glasses, hoping we would write it down. The school curtain, which is sometimes tricky, went up and down at the proper moments, operated by a couple of the Form Two boys. The audience cheered during the sword fights, which were, of course, perfectly safe. Jennifer Treece played Ophelia and in fact she looked suitably attractive.

Everything went as planned. Mr Tucker was a big hit as the gravedigger, nearly as good in his way as Clinton, although Yorick's skull, constructed by the infants, was deeply unconvincing. My only serious moment of worry was when I thought I felt an earthquake, just as the ghost made his second appearance; but no one else seemed to notice, and I suppose it may have been the weight of Gerry Speight tiptoeing across the apron, or even Brendan's fingers drumming on the back of my seat.

At the end of the play there was the line about flights of angels, after which my son got to his feet looking very much alive and happy just as the curtain began to fall. The applause was terrific and, during it, Brendan swung around, staring at me like an old friend might, and took my hand. Then he realised what he was doing, blushed a bit, and turned it into a formal handshake.

'Well done, Carol,' he said, and his voice was solemn, trembling a little. 'Congratulations,' he said, 'amazing' — as if he thought I was someone wonderful, as if he believed I had played the part myself.

Songs of My Life

He says: 'Give me something significant.'

He says: 'I've been patient. You know how patient. You have to grant that.'

I swear at him, first time ever, though I've always had the capacity.

'Tut tut,' says Maria, and he goes, 'Oh oh oh oh oh oh.'

Then he said, 'Trouble in my head,' and fell over, and Gospel Song came and sat beside him howling.

*

He asks me my dreams.

Canterbury plains, inland from the Main North Road, straight line beside pines, hills and mountains on the left, 100 m.p.h., resting his forearms on the top of the wheel while he strikes a match — Swan Vesta, you can't even buy them now.

He asks me my dreams. 100 m.p.h. and he's on about my secret life. But if it was there I don't remember. I never remembered. I just woke up recalling something about a recording studio, tapes slithering round and round and sometimes I could hear a long low sigh of relief.

'Probably a crime,' he said. 'Guilt about something. But I'm tired of the externals, tell me something.'

By now we were home again, sitting outside on the lawn. Long conversation, noises from the stockcar rally in the distance. Sprinkler working away in the early twilight — half an hour each evening we're allowed round here.

'I'm sufficiently informed,' I said. 'I have access. But anyway,'

I said, 'it's you does the songs. I thought you were supposed to tell me.'

'I'm on compassionate leave,' he says. 'As of tomorrow.'

He looks at his watch, midnight already.

'As of now.'

He walks round the side of the house, guitar on his shoulder, heading for the moonlit hills. There was wind in the garden then, Maria singing something and we went inside.

*

He travels with me, a pace or two behind, and his job is to write the songs of my life.

> It was down by the old Clutha River
> That river so famous in song
> That Colin fell in love with Maria
> But he didn't make love to her long.

'Sounds like premature whatsit,' I said, a joke but mildly anxious.

'Hell no, I was thinking, you know, that you took your pleasure and then just moved along,' said my singer, his name was Johnny Flaxbush — 'because that is what a man does, or so it seems to me, anyway, Colin.'

'Oh,' I said. 'Well, it was Queenstown. Maria was Queenstown, nice enough too, though I don't expect to see her again. Now if you don't mind just retire a little.'

You can't let art have all the victories.

*

Later that day I stood outside the Woolworths supermarket and heard this beautiful whistling, Rose of Tralee and a couple of Jim Reeves numbers. I looked around, just this old, old lady, white hair and probably plastic teeth. They're not supposed to do that, old ladies, but that was the best whistling I ever expect to hear.

*

Those were the days.

Dunedin, slate roofs the colour of marriage. Ecumenical skyline: I still like that. Spires and turrets, the tops of liftshafts.

He went by the name of Johnny Flaxbush for so long — and it never did him any harm that I could see — but one day he had these posters which said 'Pingao' and I guess he was hoping hard for better things.

> When the sun in the morning peeps over the hill
> and kisses the roses on my window sill
> then my heart fills with gladness when I hear the trill
> of the birds in the treetops on Mocking Bird Hill.

Whoah now! hold it, hold it right there, Johnny Flaxbush... Pingao...whatever your name is...those words are someone else's words, not original to you, and not linked to the life you record, which is my life. That was a big hit back in the dawn of the Fifties people called it. 1951, if I'm not mistaken.

'Oh,' he says, 'someone's angry.'

*

I went to Karitane, seeking the inspiration of fecundity. All my childhood friends were conceived at Karitane, that little town the couples visit when they marry. Nice place they have there, too, river mouth and soft ocean beach especially when the weather is appropriate. The singer occupied a tent out on the lawn.

His song was hopeless stuff, emotional turmoil I suppose, not to be reproduced here.

'People down this way say "crib",' I said to him, correcting a vocabulary item. 'Of course,' said Maria, '"crib", it's quite well known.'

Yes, I admit it, Maria was with me for a week or two, just testing the water, tip-toeing in.

*

He sings of trouble in the body, of anger in his knee. Not quite a song of himself, but getting somewhere.

I was looking for a blonde
but I ended up a failure
got mixed up with this little brunette girl's
untidy genitalia.

I asked Johnny Pingao not to sing this song in case Maria might hear.

'Is there someone?' I said. 'Someone special?'

No answer.

'Why don't you hymn the splendours of this new land of ours,' I said, 'which we are still busy building and hymning and generally conceiving.'

'Show me a reason,' he said. 'Move me with your true persuasive talk.'

I gave him topics — Zane Grey's fishing journeys to New Zealand, my developing skill on the chanter. I told him about the whole season I spent as an emergency for Zingari Richmond, a healthy team of footballers, I only ever got half of one away game. 'Professional emergency,' he said. 'Good title.'

He made a quiet song then, tender nasal chuckle of mothers talking to their children. He did not make songs about my eating preferences, my celebrated meeting with James K. Baxter, my collection of triangular stamps from San Marino.

At this period I had become the sort of person people asked to be a godfather or a pallbearer. Total strangers would come up, thinking I looked appropriate.

Explanation: absence of Maria, her overseas travels, so I missed her and waited patiently, reading John Keats aloud to him, bits of Ursula Bethell.

But he composed a song about my love of vampire movies and then, by way of contradiction, added something about my love of garlic. This song was called 'Contradiction in Terms', he presented it in Gore, and also got some airtime on Dunedin student radio. It never really flamed though, 'flamed' being how we put it in those days.

*

'Brothers and sisters?' I said to him once. But he didn't answer. His thoughts were invisible as polio.

I can still remember how those germs roamed the land, not in his songs ever, approaching at stomach height so that only adults and domestic pets were safe. They shut the town baths. My sister in the hospital, not moving much, while I was sent to the health camp at Roxburgh. Long ambulance ride through the contagious world, groceries left at the gate, and well-intentioned people waving in the distance across fences and hedges. The nervous system can only take so much noise.

'*Is* there someone?' I said.

'I tell you Colin,' he said, 'this isn't my first trip around the block.' He strummed a chord on the guitar, E7. 'And it isn't my first block.'

*

Then for a few years or so I was headmaster of a large Dunedin school. That was a good school, co-educational, and I had a personal bagpiper, a girl called Helen. She was mostly reserved for ceremonial occasions, piping me in to the senior prize-giving, and because words were no part of her business, Johnny Pingao remained a happy man. He travelled with Hank Mushroom and played in most parts of the lower South Island. He came home using the word awesome. Awesome skyline, awesome trees, awesome dimensions of the heart.

It was 1961, the year you could turn upside town.

'There are three birds in this world,' I told the assembled adolescent children. My nickname was Lunchbox, I never knew why.

'One is a hawk,' I said, 'another is a duck, and then last of all there is a hedgehog.'

I said: 'You have to decide. Which one do you want to be? I know what I would hope, but I leave it to each of you in the solitude of your soul.' I closed the large leather-bound dictionary which I opened on these occasions. It was open at 'parataxis', there in the top left corner, a word of interest to me at the time but now I admit its import escapes me.

They applauded me then, all the children, and Helen piped me out on to the fields of play.

*

I looked to see why he wasn't making music one particular morning and there was this dog — aroused, you know, moving against his knee. Nice dog, friendly dog, just restless in the desire department, the way dogs are. Well, we took on this dog and called him Gospel Song and he has been with us these last something years. Pingao saw him as a fellow minstrel, sympathetic prop. I saw him as an independent dog with his own dignity. Maria wouldn't have him in the house.

Then I won the underhand chop for the whole of New Zealand's South Island, working to a handicap of twenty-seven off dummy one.

I tried lawnmower racing, not without success, but the bit I liked most was when we all sat down afterwards and had some cup of tea.

When I moved from flairs to stovepipes, the words of Johnny Pingao celebrated this event. Was there a song called 'Platform Souls'? I don't remember.

Maria. Old hands on a young body. Otherwise, you know, totally present and correct.

*

'It's not enough of a life,' he says. 'I try,' he says, 'but there's only so much you can do with certain raw material.' He walks beside me for a moment, makes as if to touch my arm, then falls awkwardly back. 'Domesticity!' he yells, then says the word again, quieter this time, meek. 'Domesticity. Anyway, Colin, where were you, exactly, the day that they was handing out the brains?'

> Ozone hole caused
> by too much rugby football,
> big hole caused
> by going for the line.

I got a friend
comes from Takapuna
She don't sunbathe
when the weather's fine.

Usually his music will release the words, but in this particular number I think you can see that it just goes ahead and traps them.

*

When I began my own, entirely separate singing career, he made no songs about it whatsoever. Discordant noises, the thrum of an untuned guitar, a skittery run on the clarinet which he in any case had never learned to play properly. Jealousy flamed him and made him unattractive. The flamenco flourish ruled his life.

One day I walked out of the recording studio and into the arms of Maria and her mother and father and her seven brothers. The youngest brother pushed Maria forward with his goose wing, and Pingao sang about our wedding which was spoken of in many South Island towns.

I travelled to Antarctica, Alaska. I considered changing my name from Colin to something else, just what I didn't know. I had a remarkable tale to tell and I was looking for someone to tell it well and listen carefully.

But when I grew interested in the bits of Lenin's brain they have over in Moscow, Pingao was there on cue, writing a song about it. I gave him the title: '30,000 Slices'. He rhymed Lenin with some word I can't remember, then crossed it all out and did a bit of quick bush carpentry with *brain* and *Ukraine*.

Then I became Professor of Russian at Massey University, a post which had been vacant for some time so they were pleased to see me up there in the Manawatu. They were ready for Gogol and Pushkin, I guess. They must have sensed it was all over for the Cold War.

While I was at Massey there came along some women in comfortable shoes, who made no impact on me whatsoever. Maria smiled and hummed above the dishes.

While there I also began and abandoned my biography of Robert Louis Stevenson. I got him almost to Samoa twice but neither time could I make myself go on. I suppose because once he got there, inside that big happy house, *Vailima*, he would just have to die.

*

I should add that Pingao has always had these things he says, sayings, which never fail to annoy me — e.g. he will say 'Crikey', which is a perfectly good word from time to time, but coming too often it can rile or infuriate.

He will also say 'Tell me about it,' when you know he isn't really interested. When I told him for the first time about Lenin's brain, he automatically said, 'Tell me about it,' though as I say he was exceedingly keen to write the subsequent song. Ten minutes it took him. Likewise when I first used the word 'sputnik'. Tell me about it. 'Gestalt' I remember in that way, too.

In a recent development, he will also refer to me as 'someone', an exceedingly annoying habit. I might be half falling asleep, this could be in front of the television news, and he will say to Maria, 'Someone's falling asleep.' Then I flash him a glance and perhaps he will say, 'Someone's angry', and snigger.

*

'The Duke of Edinburgh Calypso': that is the one he sings all the time, especially since the long-term presence of Maria. He does it with loud persuasive feeling, too. There are lines in it, 'Two paces behind' and 'Not even on the one pound note,' which I can never remember what they rhyme with.

Not one of his songs has been in another person's mouth.

Sometimes of course I will give voice to them. It would feel wrong not to. Actually this one here is a good one which will do for many different situations:

Country gives you heartache
Country gives you pain
Country gives you back your heart
And lets you love again.

*

'Tumberling tumberling tumberling tumberling tumbleweed,' sings Maria.

'What are you thinking about?' he says. 'Colin?'

'About about about,' says Maria. 'Yes, what about?'

I try to think of something to be thinking. Maria pours another Pimm's No. 1 Cup. They say they exist, but no one I ever met has seen a Pimm's No. 2 Cup.

'Sing something,' she says.

'Me?' I said.

'You,' she said.

I looked around. No sign of Pingao. Just the dog howling in the distance — car coming fast along a gravel road.

Scandal in the elbow,
Trouble in the knee…

'I will cut out your tongue,' she says, 'and keep it in my shoe.'

I placed my hands upon her body in a sexual manner. Gospel Song settled himself behind the sofa. Rattling in his throat.

*

So do I get rid of him right here this minute, or keep him on a while? Might just be nearing time for that final, long farewell… He gets to his feet, rubbing his head. The dogs looks happy, that's a start.

'Look,' I say.

'Look, look, look,' he says. 'Tell me something significant,' he says. 'I need stuff to work with, Colin. I need the right kind of material.'

'Polio?' I say, and he says: 'No.'

'Pregnant woman?'

'No, no, no, no, no!'

He starts to say something. Twilight. Whole width of the room between us.

'There was once three birds, this big hawk and this duck and...'

'No,' I say, 'Stop! Stop at once, Johnny Pingao! Storics arc outlawed round here, you know that. They take too long.'

'Look, it's a joke,' he says, 'just a joke about a hedgehog.'

Voice pleading, eyes pleading, dog looking breathless in the background.

'A *joke*.'

Maria comes and stands beside me. 'Tumberling tumberling... hic.'

A joke. Well now. A joke.

'Just a joke, Colin... Like, like, what's the difference between an egg and a beetroot?'

A beetroot? An egg and a beetroot?

But jokes are too difficult: I'm getting someone else for that.

South Pacific

1

Two days before he left New Zealand Allen received a phone call. It was a woman, but not a voice he recognised.

'I hope it's not too late at night,' said the caller, 'and this is probably a mistake but I've been trying to get up courage all evening.'

It was ten o'clock.

'Are you there?' she said.

'Yes,' he said. 'Who is this?' It occurred to him that this was how Americans talked, that he was acting.

'Oh, I'm *very* sorry. I think perhaps I've made a mistake.'

'Pardon?' said Allen.

'You're not the Samaritans, are you?'

'This is a private number. Was it the Samaritans you were trying to call?'

'I feel extremely silly,' said the woman. 'It's taken me a week to get to the point, and then I get a wrong number.'

She had an educated voice, a speech lessons voice.

'It's all right,' he said.

'Actually I've found out I'm dying,' the woman said. 'It's not at all fair for me to be telling you this, I realise that. But I had it all worked out. I was going to say it right away when they answered.'

Allen made a noise. A shrugging noise in his throat.

'Is your number quite near theirs? I suppose you get a lot of calls like this.'

'No,' he said. 'It hasn't happened before.'

'I've been sitting here looking at photographs. It's silly. I had them all in a shoebox.'

For some reason Allen thought of his passport photograph. He had had a new one taken a couple of months earlier, colour, yet somehow it looked pale and dated.

'It has one of those polysyllabic names,' said the woman. 'I suppose you'd like me to hang up?'

'No,' he said. 'It's all right. It really is.'

'You've got a lovely voice, did you know that? It seems a shame to let you go.' The woman paused. 'Are those children I can hear in the background?'

'I don't think so.' The kids were in bed. 'It might be a bad line.'

'I'm finding it quite hard to hear you,' said the woman. 'Would you mind holding on a minute? I'll get the children to turn the radio down.'

He waited, pressing the receiver hard against his ear. Could he hear a radio in the distance? Children's voices? People quarrelling? He could not tell.

From time to time Jean came through to the hall with an inquiring look on her face. He waved her away. Once she pointed to her watch.

He held on for fourteen minutes, waiting for the dying woman to return. Then he hung up.

2

London was cold — grey and puzzling. People bumped into one another on the footpaths, they clustered in shivering groups around map-books. Black rubbish bags were stacked against shopfronts, taxis nudged their way along the streets. He had found a small hotel a few blocks from the British Museum. His room was on the top floor, with a view of roofs and chimney pots. Mary Poppins stuff.

The roof of the building opposite was buried in rubble — timber plasterboard, lumps of plumbing and splintered brick. Men lowered it all through scaffolding to a skip below. A sign on the front of the building said *Prestige Office Space.* Along the road another sign said *Superior Office Space.*

His first act had been to get out the South Pacific board. He put New Zealand in place, in the picture, then propped the game on top of the dressing table. Evidence of home. On the calendar above his bed he circled the departure date — making sure he was sure of it. There was something wrong with the calendar. The legend read, 'March — the Gardens at Crathes Castle, Grampian'. But the picture was of Ben Nevis, snow-clad, against a background of cloud.

He woke with a start at three in the morning. In the thin light from the bedlamp he searched for the book Jean had given him. *The Envoy from Mirror City*. It was part of the life story of Janet Frame, the New Zealand writer. It was about the time she had spent overseas — a suitable gift for travellers.

He leafed through the pages. Janet Frame was in Andorra, in the Pyrenees. She had become engaged to an Italian, El Vici Mario, who lodged in the same house as she did. They had walked together in the mountains, and he had said to her, *'Voulez-vous me marier, moi?'* El Vici could speak three languages. He had a blue-and-white bicycle, picked grapes and had fought against the fascists. Janet Frame did not say yes but she did not say no either. She did not know how to. She told El Vici that she had to go to London before the marriage, that there were 'things to see to'. She would be back soon. She bought a return ticket — but she never meant to return.

Allen marked his place; he yawned.

Deep in Andorra, deep in Allen's sleep, El Vici waited patiently for Janet Frame. He whispered to himself in French, Spanish and Italian. He was a tall, stooped figure with two-toned shoes, and he wheeled his blue-and-white bicycle along the roads of Europe, road after road, until one day, there he was, wheeling his bicycle through the small arcade behind New Zealand House. El Vici gazed into the window of the little bookshop. He saw a display of books by Janet Frame. He shivered in the cold.

Allen had just finished serving a customer when El Vici pushed open the shop door.

'Prego' said El Vici. He was holding the South Pacific board. *'Dov'è Nuova Zelanda?'*

El Vici's nicotine-stained finger hovered above the expanse of blue. Allen felt sorry for him. Another traveller lost in a foreign city.

He took El Vici's finger and dipped it in a jar of Vegemite.

'Taste that,' he said. 'Go on, try it.'

3

A man in the trade section at New Zealand House said to him across a desk that he should really have made some sort of preliminary appointment before he left home. He seemed pleased to be talking, though. He introduced himself as Mike Bekeris. He drummed his fingers on the game board.

'Lots of blue,' he said. 'South Pacific, eh?'

'Well, the real game mostly takes place in the players' consultations and so on.' Allen felt he had to offer something. 'It's a role-playing game, really. The board's as much a matter of focus as anything. Every time you discover a new country you can place it on the board, physically put it there. So while you have to work with given names, you can build up the map as you go along. We've tried to mimic the actual conditions of exploration. In fact, you could play a whole game through without even discovering New Zealand.'

A girl put her head around the door and said, 'That's all right about Martin Crowe.'

Mike Bekeris said to Allen: 'Not quite my sort of thing, personally, board games. But then your problem isn't going to be selling it to me.'

'No,' said Allen.

'I'll be straight with you, Mr Douglas.' Mike Bekeris leant across the desk like an actor in a play. 'A lot of people come in here in your position — cottage industry sort of thing — and there isn't a great deal of return for anyone on the time put in. In any case, my hands are tied. I can give you, oh, half an hour, but then you have to decide just how serious you want our involvement to be.'

'Fair enough,' said Allen.

'Now I take it you aren't in production yet — well you can't be, or you'd have something more finished to show me. So what are your options? I'd say you can try and market direct, or you can pass the whole thing across to one of the big companies.'

'How do you mean?'

'Well, you would license Waddingtons, let us say, to produce and market the game in certain territories. I won't be telling you anything new there. Your problem is that Waddingtons might not see much future for a game like this in Europe or North America; and they might want to sell back into Australasia. If they want to see you at all.'

'We thought we would try to do our own marketing at home,' said Allen.

'So: direct marketing. But remember that over here you'd be chasing your tail inside a huge market looking for the specialist market. You'd certainly need someone on the ground, so you'd be looking at a fairly big outlay in the first instance. So maybe that means you have to go after sponsorship.'

'You mean here?' said Allen. 'Or at home?'

'Actually, the thing you have to decide,' said Mike Bekeris, 'is whether you want us to come any further down the track with you. We've moved on to a firm cost-recovery system these days: I don't come free on the tax-payer. So if you'd like us to do a bit of preliminary work — e.g. try to set up appointments with game manufacturers — then you have to commit yourself to a bit of expenditure. However you go, you can still write off 60 per cent of your trip as product development.'

Allen stared at a wall poster — 'Auckland: City of Sails'. The blue slashed with sheets of white. He felt that Mike Bekeris was daring him to do something quite outrageous. But what, exactly?

'Why don't you think about it,' said Mike Bekeris, 'and give me a call over the next few days?'

The cold ate into everything. Sheets of paper flapped slowly down the Haymarket. Allen walked up through Soho, past restaurants and sex shops. It was mid-afternoon, a respectable time of day, and Soho seemed more discreet, more muted than he remembered. There were no posters outside the cinemas he passed. No one called softly from the mouths of hostess bars.

Sex was more prominent in the Virgin Games Shop in Oxford Street. At least, he found himself noticing the sex games first. Libido, Foreplay, Dr Ruth's Game of Good Sex. They seemed to be versions of strip poker, overlaid with questions of the Trivial Pursuit kind. Dr Ruth promised 'interactive cards'.

The fantasy games bred among themselves at the back of the shop. Dungeons and Dragons, Talisman, Runequest, Call of Cthulhu, Thieves' World, Star Trek, Sorcerer's Cave...Near them were the history games. You could fight every campaign of the American Civil War, you could join battle with Napoleon across the map of Europe. Among the World War II games, one called Pacific War caught his eye. But it turned out to involve America and Japan fighting the battles of 1941-45.

He asked an assistant if the shop had any travel or exploration games and was pointed to a display of a game called Capital Adventure — 'a travel game for people going places'. Some skill seemed to be involved in choosing the best air route between one capital city and the next. 'Take calculated risks,' said the box, 'and face the dangers that every global traveller meets.'

But there was no overlap with South Pacific.

He looked for the assistant again and described South Pacific, pretending it was a game he had read about somewhere and would be interested to buy.

'Sounds interesting,' said the assistant. It was the sort of thing they would want to have in stock, but he had never seen it. Did Allen know who made it?

'A New Zealand company, I think.'

'Ah, well.'

'If I get the details,' said Allen, 'I could drop you a note.'

'We'd surely appreciate it. We try to be comprehensive. I *think* there used to be something called Columbus. Discover America sort of thing.'

Back at the hotel Allen pushed open the door of the tiny guest lounge. A wall heater beamed its warmth on a Bengali family who sat in front of the television. One of them, an elderly woman, held a badminton racquet across her knees. Allen watched for a few minutes — Tottenham and Arsenal in extra time — then went up to his room.

His bed had been made, the cover turned back. Two hairclips lay on the pillow. He stared at them, at the shiny insect legs. He felt for his wallet in his pocket.

He looked out Monika's number and went down to the coin-box in the hall. She answered the telephone herself. She had been expecting to hear, she said. Jean had sent a letter: they must get together.

'I'm afraid it wouldn't work for you to come round here,' she said. 'But I wonder if we mightn't do something on Saturday? I can bring Lark. We can make a bit of a day of it. The thing is, I haven't got all that much money at the moment.'

4

They met under an AIDS billboard outside the London Dungeon. Allen insisted on buying the tickets. Lark was half-price, in any case.

'I'll write you off as a business expense,' he said.

'I hope you don't mind starting off here,' Monika said as they walked through the clinical half darkness. 'Lark's been wanting to come for ages. I'm sure it'll be dreadful. Like the Chamber of Horrors.'

She had a green jewelled stud in the side of her nose. It glinted, catching the candlelight as they moved around.

'Are we under the river?' asked Lark. 'Bet we are.' She ran ahead.

They strolled among the unconvincing horrors of tourist London, passing from a scene of Druid sacrifice to a life-size model of St George, who was strapped to an X-shaped cross and bled where his flesh had been scraped by jagged combs. Further on, blood poured from the neck of Mary Queen of Scots like water from a playground drinking fountain. Behind a window live rats scurried about a skull.

'Poor things,' said Lark. 'Aren't they cute?'

'It's a *plague* display,' said Allen. 'You're supposed to be frightened.'

Beside the skull was a bowl filled with grain. He could just make out the lettering of the word DOG on the bowl's surface.

They paused in front of Sawney Beane, the Scottish cannibal. He and his family had lived for twenty-five years in a cave near Edinburgh. They killed unsuspecting passers-by, cutting up their bodies and pickling them. They chuckled horribly over their evening meal. After they had been captured, the men were castrated; their arms and feet were cut off, and they were left to bleed to death. The notice said that the women 'were burned in three fires.'

'Why?' said Lark. 'Why did they do that to the women?'

'Witch paranoia,' said Monika. 'They thought the women had all the real power.'

'Your father would know,' said a woman, tugging a small boy after her. But she was talking about something else.

They sat in a cafeteria at the Barbican.

'I thought it would be *frightening*,' said Lark.

Monika fingered the bone pendant which Allen had brought her from Jean.

'It's designed not to be,' said Monika. 'You're supposed to get a taste of terror but without the reality.'

She looked at Allen as if to indicate that she was saying one thing to Lark and another to him.

'Listen,' said Lark. She read out a witch's spell from one of the postcards Allen had bought.

'To win the love of a woman who does not want you, thread a needle with her hair and run it through the fleshiest limb of a dead man.'

She looked at her mother's cropped hair.

'You're safe, Mummy. No one would ever get your hair through the needle. It's far too short.'

'First find your dead man,' said Monika. 'Then we'll see.'

Allen remembered her taking his hand in a Greek restaurant in

Camden Town, years ago. She had long hair then. Jean was there. His fingers were clenched up inside his palm. She unbent his fingers, one by one, then placed his hand flat, palm down, on the table. 'That's advice,' she said, 'not a proposition.'

'I think you should send your children the scariest ones,' said Lark.

Outside it was snowing. The snow fell into a long rectangular pond of water. There were ducks on the water, and beyond it was the sixteenth-century church of St Giles-without-Cripplegate where, said the guidebook, Oliver Cromwell had been married.

Lark went out to stand in the snow. She waved at them through the window. But the snow wasn't going to settle.

'Eight years old,' said Allen. 'Amazing.'

'Jean hasn't seen her since she was five weeks old.'

Lark waved through the window.

'But she had to go back,' said Allen. 'We went back together. She'll be across on the next trip. If this game works out.'

'South Pacific,' said Monika.

'South Pacific,' said Allen.

A pale leaflet lay on the floor outside his bedroom door.

'Rubber: the fantasy; Love Potions; Pillow Talk; The Mistress: I'm waiting to talk to you!' There were drawings of girls in lingerie, and a list of names, each with a telephone number. *Saucy Girls!*

He folded the sheet and tucked it into his pocket. A souvenir.

Next day, Sunday, he walked in the City, drifting through anaemic sunshine. At St Paul's he bought a tiny crystal bell for Jean. There was a giftshop just inside the main entrance.

In his hotel bedroom he played a game of South Pacific. But his mind failed to concentrate. Player A discovered Samoa but failed to control his crew, who introduced the native population to alcohol, then a few moves later gave them syphilis. Player B drifted in the blue.

Allen lay on the bed and masturbated. He would not call Mike Bekeris.

He tried to imagine the voice of a saucy girl but could only imagine silence. But it was all right. The light caught the jewel in the side of Monika's nose as she lowered her head towards him, and her hair, long, abundant, fell forward, shielding her face.

5

He spent his last two days staying with one of his father's cousins, Margaret. Margaret's house lay directly beneath the flight-path at Gatwick. She could tell one kind of aircraft from another by the engine noise as they came in to land. On top of the television she kept a photograph of her late husband.

It was an amiable duty visit. Allen gave news of home, and Margaret was happy to leave him largely to himself. He went for walks, jotted down notes for a possible game on Antarctic exploration, glanced at a chapter from the Janet Frame book. He would leave the book with Margaret.

There was news of a ferry disaster. A boat had capsized sailing out of a Belgian harbour. As many as 200 were feared drowned. Margaret settled in her chair in front of the television, holding the remote control, flicking between channels.

Allen rang a saucy girl. He pressed the phone close to his ear.

A voice welcomed him to International Celebrity Line. He was through to Erica Croft.

Erica Croft explained that as a top model she visited many exciting places. Today she was on location in the South Pacific.

'We're shooting one of those chocolate bar commercials — you know, the desert island bit where you discover the treasure chest full of chewy bars. It's lovely out here, with the bleached golden sands and palm trees and gently rippling waves.'

She said that since they had a break in shooting, she would say something about some of the other countries she had been to.

'Once I went to shoot a calendar with a few other girls in North Africa. We were hoping to get a lovely tan and come back with great stories and lovely pictures, but the whole trip was an absolute disaster. There were sandstorms on the beach and it poured with rain. All the girls got bitten by insects.

'Another trip I went on earlier this year was to Cyprus, to shoot a commercial for babies' nappies. There were twenty-five babies plus all the parents plus all the lighting plus the cameraman — all in one tiny room which was actually a ballet school. Well you can imagine the chaos in there. That was another trip that turned out to be a bit of a disaster. But they managed to make the commercial in the end, it came out looking ever so good.

'Before I go, let me just tell you today's secret. I'd really like to learn to fly.'

Allen pressed the receiver to his ear. 'Don't forget to call tomorrow when I'll be revealing even more about myself,' said Erica Croft. Then there was music, then the line went dead.

6

London — Bombay — Perth — Melbourne — Auckland

He was next to a young couple. The man was Chilean; he looked like a teenager. The woman was Scottish and spoke for both of them. They were going to Australia: a new start. They played Scrabble, the husband and wife, on a small magnetic board. The man kept consulting a paperback dictionary.

Just after dawn they landed at Bombay. Transiting passengers strolled past a line of shops. Stall owners stood in their doorways with heads held sideways, squinting. The terminal building was fairly new, but it held an evening darkness. Allen was pleased when the reboarding call was made.

The plane taxied out to the end of the runway, swung laboriously about and began to gather speed. The seats next to Allen were empty. What had happened to the young couple? Through the window he could see army vehicles in the distance, painted in camouflage greens.

Then he felt himself thrown forward. The engines shrieked, the cabin shook. The overhead baggage doors flapped open, trembling like absurd wings.

Allen gripped the armrests. The plane was braking, skidding.

He could see other passengers hunched forward, arms shielding their heads in what, it half dawned on him, was the recommended crash position.

The plane bumped off the runway, lurched to a halt. The engines stopped.

It would be a bomb. Someone was talking in a high voice towards the back of the cabin. A baby was crying.

Then the captain was speaking over the intercom. He apologised. A warning light had come up on a panel, probably nothing at all, but of course better to be safe than sorry. They wouldn't be leaving for a while now, he was afraid; it was going to be some time before the brakes cooled.

'Let me reassure you, however. There was plenty of runway out in front when I applied the brakes. But I do apologise for the rather sudden stop.'

The plane limped across to a remote corner of the airfield. An army vehicle kept it company. Beyond the tarmac there was a kind of shantytown. Faces stared through a perimeter fence.

People talked. The cabin crew brought drinks. An hour later the captain made a further announcement. Several tyres had blown out during the braking operation. A hunt was on for replacements, which were proving hard to find. He was going across to airport control to talk to London just to see if regulations might not be stretched a little — not, of course, beyond the bounds of passenger safety.

Much later, it seemed, an airline official came on board to announce that passengers were now able to proceed to the terminal. But of course they might stay aboard the carrier if they wished. This would be the only chance to disembark, however, and departure might still be several hours. He wanted to remind passengers that the terminal was air-conditioned.

About two-thirds of the cabin filed out to the waiting coaches. Allen remained in his seat. The plane was real, the terminal a dark imaginary place. The exit doors had been opened so that a breeze might circulate in the cabin. But there was no breeze; it was hot beyond belief, the deep insistent heat of early afternoon.

Allen made his way to the front of the plane and looked out the door. At the foot of the steps were several armed soldiers.

A few passengers stood halfway down the steps. They craned their necks to catch sight of the wheels of the 747. An Indian passenger stood at the top of the steps.

'Nothing doing,' he said. 'You can go to the bottom step, but if your foot should touch the tarmac, then I believe these men may shoot you.'

He introduced himself. He was Mr Murugesar. 'My wife is back there,' he said. 'Keeping to her seat.'

Mr Murugesar lived in Sydney. He was an importer. 'Things of all kinds.' His wife had many relations in Bombay. These were the people they had been visiting. 'But they are hopeless people. They will never get away.' Mr Murugesar gestured towards the invisible city, apparently including all of its citizens in the sweep of his arm.

Allen could hear a flight steward explaining that permission had come through to use Air India tyres. There was only a small difference in specifications. But it would still be some time before they could begin removing the damaged ones: they were still too hot.

Mr Murugesar sat beside Allen and spoke to him of New Zealand. One day he hoped to go there. 'All of the South Pacific,' he said. 'The islands and so forth.' England, of course, where Allen had been, he knew England well.

'The sounding cataract haunted me like a passion,' said Mr Murugesar. 'Little lines of sportive wood run wild. Tintern Abbey, did you visit there?'

Allen explained that he had only been to London. A marketing trip. He talked about the board game.

'Most interesting,' said Mr Murugesar. 'We are brothers of the road.' He lowered his voice and whispered to Allen that someone had said that a limousine collecting a government minister had exploded outside the airport. 'But I think you will find this is not true,' he said.

Allen stood halfway down the steps. About thirty men were gathered around the lumpy black tyres. They prodded and gesticulated, shouting at each other.

'Well at least they're making some show of getting on with it,' said a tall Australian. He said that the real problem was that the cabin crew would soon come to the end of their shift. 'So none of the current lot will be allowed to fly out of Bombay. They'll be scouring the city for a stand-by crew. Cross everything you've got.'

Mr Murugesar was also pessimistic. Nine hours had passed; soon they would all be taken into the city. He read to Allen from a guidebook, eyeing him shyly from time to time.

'From Bombay the first Indian locomotive steamed down to Thana in 1853.'

'Bombay turns out the largest number of movies in the world.'

'Bombay is a colourful racial and linguistic mosaic.'

Mr Murugesar described the Mahalakshmi Temple. 'Goddess of Prosperity. But the city owes its name to Goddess Mumba-devi.'

He flipped through the book. 'Ah! This will interest New Zealanders.'

He held the book before him in both hands.

'Aarey Milk Colony, perhaps the largest in Asia, set amidst gardens. From the Observation Pavilion on a hillock near the entrance, one can see the process of pasteurisation and bottling of milk. This is an ideal picnic spot. Cottages available.'

Mr Murugesar lowered Allen's flight tray. He placed the book gently upon it.

'Now,' he said, '*The Gateway to India*. My gift to you.'

Passengers were filing back into the cabin. A new crew moved about, crisp and pressed. The young Chilean and his Scottish wife appeared. They smiled as though nothing had happened.

Then the plane was airborne. The new captain gave a flight time to Perth, and a cruising altitude. He invited passengers to adjust their watches. The drinks trolley came. A meal came. The young couple played Scrabble. The man made the word *sailer* on the board; he held the dictionary up in front of his wife and pointed.

Allen watched the film. Robert Redford and a beautiful woman were investigating crooked art dealers in New York.

He fell asleep and then he was in Auckland, clouds and sails. But it was London, and he was walking in the City — following someone, or being followed, he could not tell. Snow fell into the concrete moats of the Barbican. El Vici rode past on his bicycle, waving slowly. *'Dov'è Nuova Zelanda?'*

But the streets were deserted. He was wading through the cold and darkness of a winter afternoon.

He began to drift with the cold. It came in clouds, leaking from walls and domes, from tower blocks, from the stone of ancient churches. He felt himself dissolving, consciousness without form, blurred and indefinite. He drifted in his blood, he seeped away.

Now the damp pores of stone opened to accept him. Atom by atom, they took him in. He was mist melting into water, dampness sinking through sand. Soon no trace of him would remain.

Yet there was something which was not taken in. He could feel it — a stubborn part of himself which would not dissolve, would not budge, would not be absorbed in stone. He reached out. He touched it. He touched it gently, with his misty hand. It was his erection, which he woke to find himself holding, high above the Indian Ocean, as the 747 reduced power and began the slow descent towards Perth.

Pengucapan Puisi
KUALA LUMPUR
Poetry Reading

Mr. Bill Manhire,
Department of English,
Victoria University of Wellington,
P.O. Box 600,
Wellington,
New Zealand.

Our ref.: DBP-4/36 K.5 (173)

Date: September 24th. 1990.

Dear Manhire,

THE THIRD KUALA LUMPUR WORLD POETRY READING 1990:
PARTICIPANT'S TICKET

Your ticket is ready! Thank you very much to Malaysia Airlines our main sponsor, with its charm and hospitable has come forward to fly you to Kuala Lumpur, The City of Light to participate in this festival.

2. Your ticket is already cleared and please re-confirm it and do follow your right date to depart for Kuala Lumpur. At the Subang Airport International (Malaysia) you will be welcomed by a team from the secretariat. Transport to hotel is waiting for you. Although some of you would arrive before 25th. October, please do not worry, we are looking and pay for your accommodation and food.

3. "SELAMAT DATANG" is Malaysian way to greet you poets of the World. Please come and enjoy every moment of this Kuala Lumpur World Poetry Festival. This is our own festival and we are together responsible to enlighten it.

Until then, warm regards and love.

Sincerely yours,

Ahmad Kamal Abdullah

(AHMAD KAMAL ABDULLAH, Kemala)
Secretary-general,
Third Kuala Lumpur World Poetry Reading 1990,
for Director General.

c.c.: i. The Chairman.
ii. The Deputy Chairman.

Wings of Gold: A Week Among Poets

A few years ago one of the present authors, then in Malaysia, was approached by a visiting New Zealand Member of Parliament. 'I have just two important questions for you,' he said. 'What is really going on in this country, and what are the names of the two main types of dress worn by Chinese women here?'

R.S. MILNE and DIANE K. MAUZY, *Malaysia: Tradition, Modernity, and Islam*

High above the Australian interior I sit in a Malaysian Airlines DC10 — knees under my chin, *Wings of Gold* on my knees. I am on my way to the third Kuala Lumpur World Poetry Reading. I open and re-read the letter that came with my flight ticket.

I am faintly confused about my name. In this letter I am addressed as Manhire, but an earlier fax from the organisers came to Billo Manhire. They are probably confused because they had been banking on getting Cilla McQueen. Cilla has had to pull out in favour of her theatre piece, *Red Rose Café*, which is about to première in Dunedin. But the Billo is rather good. Friends have debated its appropriateness: does it suggest a failed Hobbit or a mild abrasive? Or is Billo built on the model of the missing Cilla? 'From Cilla to Billo' — it has a certain ring. There might be an essay on New Zealand poetry here.

The in-flight magazine, *Wings of Gold*, is written mostly in English. Alas, the only item written entirely in Bahasa Malaysia is the three-page spread devoted to the Kuala Lumpur World

Poetry Reading, and I understand none of it, although the word *puisi* has begun to acquire some meaning. Further on, a section called *Dateline Malaysia* explains that there are two particularly exciting events taking place in Kuala Lumpur in the last week of October. One is the World Poetry Reading. 'More than forty international poets are expected to take part in the Third Kuala Lumpur World Poetry Reading. Twenty-two of the countries confirmed are Jordan, West Germany, Turkey, Soviet Union, Belgium and France.'

The other event is the World Body Building Championships.

The guidebooks give you facts: 330,000 square kilometres, only 40 per cent of it in Peninsular Malaysia, where about 85 per cent of the population live. The population is about 14 million; 54 per cent are Malays and other indigenous people; Chinese are 35 per cent, Indians 10 per cent. Freedom of worship is guaranteed in Malaysia, but it is essentially an Islamic nation. The constitution even defines a Malay as a person who habitually speaks Malay (Bahasa Malaysia), conforms to Malay custom, and follows Islam. And although Kuala Lumpur now calls itself the City of Light (1990 is 'Visit Malaysia Year'), the name in fact means Muddy Estuary. The city is built where a bunch of nineteenth-century tin prospectors set up camp at the confluence of two rivers. (These days the rivers flow through huge concrete drainage channels — gigantic versions of Dunedin's Leith Stream.)

Before I left New Zealand, long before the cabin crew turned on the musak ('Harbour Lights') and demonstrated safety procedures, I asked people about Malaysia. One friend told me about the *bumiputra* policies. *Bumiputra* means 'sons of the soil' and Malaysia has a range of measures designed to discriminate in favour of the indigenous peoples, mainly the ethnic Malays, so that they can gain a more equitable share of the nation's wealth. There are Malay privileges in business licences, land ownership, government jobs, tertiary opportunities. Someone else explained that Malaysia was one of the powerhouses of the new Asia: its economic success made the New Zealand of Roger Douglas look absurd.

But most people made dark jokes about drugs. One night I turned on a BBC television play, *Among Barbarians*, about young English drug smugglers in Malaysia. I thought there might be some establishing shots, a few images to give the feel of the place: mosques, perhaps, or majestic rainforest. But all I could see was an anxious British family arriving at an airport, then a hotel. I went back to marking end-of-year exams. 'Katherine Mansfield talked of seeing her world in glimpses. How does she make such apparently significant moments worth writing about?' After about an hour I flicked on the set again, just in time to see two bodies plummeting through the hangman's trapdoor.

My arrival card says:

BE FOREWARNED
DEATH FOR DRUG TRAFFICKERS UNDER
MALAYSIAN LAW

And just as we land there is a brief announcement about drug smuggling. 'Such an offence will carry a mandatory sentence. Thank you.'

It is raining as we land, 7.40 p.m. local time in a steaming, equatorial world. Two men stand around the baggage claim, both wearing face masks, like surgeons in an operating theatre. A young German drifts through the arrival hall asking people to lend him his airfare home. I am luckier than him. Someone holds a sheet of paper saying 'Manhire'. I have been looked for, I am safe, I do not worry. There are several young men to meet me, and even another poet who has just stepped off a flight from Brunei. One man does all the talking: he is small, all in black, and keeps breaking into nervous, high-pitched laughter. He reminds me of Joel Gray in *Cabaret*.

'Mr Bill,' he says, laughing and thrusting an envelope into my hand. 'Hundred ringgit. Is all for you from us. You sign.'

He has a form which says I have received the money. I sign it. Malaysia will turn out to be a land of forms and form-filling.

'You are at Holiday Inn ok? Sharing the rooms. This is how it is happening, ok?' There is an edge to his voice. 'OK?'

I must look faintly puzzled. So he adds: 'Englishman won't. Sebastian! But you are not Englishman, Mr Bill, you New Zealand.' A wild laugh leaves his body in high little ripples. He stops laughing and cries, 'English poet!' Then he says something in Bahasa Malaysia to his colleagues. They all laugh — a sort of anxious hysteria. Then we are in a car, on a motorway, and the neon signs say Guinness, Toyota, Hilton.

At the Holiday Inn, someone darts away with my bag. Someone else tells me that I am sharing a room with a Thai poet. But there is only one key, the Thai poet already has it, and anyway we must go to the dinner! Moments later I am sitting at a table. It is some sort of banquet hall. In fact, many people sit at many tables, there is one of those low ceilings made of smoky steel. The table is set with jugs of water and glasses of orange cordial — which for some reason remind me of a childhood holiday at Pounawea.

I am with a bunch of young Malay men and the poet from Brunei. Food is brought and we smile at one another between mouthfuls. Someone manages to explain that the dinner is sponsored by the Ministry of Tourism and Culture. The Minister of Tourism himself is here. He is pleased: his government has just been re-elected. The idea of poetry as news is news to me — whatever Ezra Pound said about it. But photographers race about the banquet hall, darting out of the way of the arc lights and cables trailed by television news teams. The room is full of poets and photo opportunities. The Minister makes a long speech in Bahasa Malaysia. People chat and sip their orange cordial. The Minister appends a brief English summary. He uses phrases like 'the betterment of mankind'. He suggests that poets should 'highlight positive values'. In a world which is too individualistic, he says, poets 'can act as the stabilising factor that contributes to human development'.

Then the Minister sets off around the room. He shakes hands with the international guest poets, who seem mostly to be clustered at tables masked by a couple of pillars on the far side of the hall. The Minister is trailed by light: subordinates, press photographers and the television crews. Many of the poets are armed with their own cameras and they too join the media throng. By the time the Minister reaches my table, his hand extended, half the banquet hall is travelling with him.

There is entertainment. A Malay band plays music; elegantly costumed men and women dance. Like all the Malay bands I meet during the week, this one has fiddle, flute, piano accordion and an astonishing variety of drums. It is like an Irish pub band with a huge percussion section. The players are all young, except for an elderly bald man on fiddle. His fiddle is painted blue and white, like waves and ocean, like (I think later) doves and clouds crossing a perfect sky. The music itself is both background and foreground: familiar and strange, insistent, swooping through the room and about the heads of the international poets who crowd around the band with cameras.

I meet Kemala, the author of my letter of invitation. He leads me about the room, introducing me to the poets of the world. I hear names but remember countries. Sri Lanka is here, and Turkey. So are Korea, Canada, Nepal, Switzerland, Japan, England, China. Australia is an amiable, slow-motion Tom Shapcott, who is also just off the plane. Then there are Jordan, Romania, Philippines, Germany — and Pakistan, who will pursue and persecute me during the week with reports on the progress of the New Zealand cricket tour. Also there are Egypt, a couple of Norways, and a small delegation of very big poets from Yugoslavia. No sign of America. I meet my room-mate, the Thai poet, Prayom Songthong. The prayer and song in his name help me remember it. Prayom is in his late 50s or early 60s — courtly, gentle, softly spoken.

I have entered a situation familiar to all New Zealanders who go away from home. I have none of Prayom's language; he has a little of mine. But it is surprising how much we can talk about. Back in New Zealand it is 4.30 a.m., but in Room 1613 in the Holiday Inn Kuala Lumpur City Centre, it is 11.30 at night, and Prayom explains that he likes to have television on late while he writes. 'Mostly letters,' he says. 'TV and write.' I climb into bed, anyway, half aware of an American car chase. I close my eyes and Prayom writes in his notebook. Then there is news. I sleep, or imagine I sleep, very briefly. When I wake, half-an-hour later, I can hear the over-excited music that signals television news. What is happening in Malaysia round about midnight? Ah, there are the bodybuilders, lines and lines of them, meeting the Prime Minister, bursting out of their jackets. Then there is something about the new Malaysia cabinet, then something about (I think) Tasmania, then something else altogether: a room full of people sitting at tables, and the Minister of Tourism, Dattuk Sabbaruddin Chik, reaching across to shake my hand.

A Mysterious Poem

From afar we saw the sea flickered
in a festival of lights. Fishermen
told us fluorescent lamps attracted sotongs
to the hook or 'candat' at the end of the line.
The hook reflected in the water.

Sotongs were curious with the way
lights played on the hook. A sotong
wobbled up from the deep
and lingered by it. I waited
till it was close enough

when I jerked the line up
along with the sotong
whose limbs were tangled up
by the hook. The sotong discharged
black liquid all over my face.

* * *

26 OCTOBER

The morning paper, the *New Straits Times*, slides under the door. There is a lot of stuff about the recent Malaysian election and the divvying up of perks and power — who will be in the new cabinet, and so on. And one fascinating sentence: 'Penang is set to enjoy greater development as the new State Government is composed of intellectuals.' There is a list of Ministers: they all have PhDs.

New Zealand is there on the international page, too. Even in Kuala Lumpur, things look disastrous for Labour.

I bump into a blackboard in the lobby which says there is a registration room for poets. I find it and register. This involves paying a sum of US$100.00 — a good deal more than the 100 ringgits I was given at the airport. I am given an extraordinary folder. It is imitation leather; it has a clipboard and many pockets, and there are many things in the pockets: a 52-page full-colour programme, car stickers promoting the World Poetry Reading, various small booklets and invitations.

I discover that the detail of the formal readings is already settled. I am to read 'Zoetropes' and 'Megasin' (*sic*) — the last poems I would think to read to a non-English audience normally. The organisers had asked for sample poems, and I faxed them through from Wellington at the last minute simply because they were short. Fortunately I can worry about this later. My first reading duty will be in Shah Alam late tomorrow afternoon. I'm not down to read in tonight's big opening ceremony in the Kuala Lumpur City Hall. Phew!

WE WILL PROCEED TO CITY HALL AUDITORIUM AT 7.30 PM. PLEASE GET INTO THE BUS FIVE MINUTES EARLIER.
YOU WILL READ IN YOUR OWN LANGUAGE AND IT WILL BE FOLLOWED BY MALAY TRANSLATION. NO XX INTRODUCTORY SPEECHES ALLOWED. PLEASE GO STRAIGHT WITH YOUR READING. ONE POEM ONLY JUST AS STATED IN THE PROGRAMME BOOKLET. THANK YOU FOR YOUR KIND COOPERATION.

KEMALA
Secretary-general

INTRODUCTIONS

At 3.30, there is an introductions session. 'At the Introductory Meeting, we will introduce you one by one to the other participants. The Director General of Dewan Bahasa dan Pustaka, the principal sponsor of this Festival, will give greetings. Foreign as well as local journalists will freely interview you at this meeting. We appreciate your cooperation. High Tea (consisting of various tasty local dishes) will be served at 5.00 p.m.' The New Zealand High Commissioner is coming to this session to present books of New Zealand poetry to the Festival organisers. About twenty minutes it should take, one of his staff thinks. It's not clear if I will have to speak.

In the event everyone will have to speak.

The Introductory session begins with a very long speech in Bahasa Malaysia from the Director of Dewan Bahasa to a room containing almost no Malays but many uncomprehending foreign poets.

Then a Yugoslav woman makes a very long speech in Serbo-Croatian. She is the editor of an anthology of Malaysia poetry translated into Serbo-Croatian. This strikes me as a wonderful cross-city bus — though as the speech goes on, I realise that the speaker, like many Yugoslavs, is Islamic, and that the poetry bus she travels on is powered by an engine called Islamic Revival. All the same, it makes you realise how few and how predictable are New Zealand's international connections. The editor's speech is then translated into English. Then three poems are read in Serbo-Croatian; then there are English translations. Then there is a long speech of thanks in several languages. There is a formal presentation of the anthology. The editor shakes the hand of the Director of the Dewan Bahasa. The room is suddenly full of photographers; and there are the television crews again.

Now one by one the poets mount the rostrum and introduce themselves. There's competition between the guest poets at flattering the hosts. Something both ingratiating and patronising is going on, but in a long-winded way both sides end up satisfied. 'It is good to make love in Malay,' says a Malay poet, proud of his language. 'I have tried it and it works.' I say something fatuous about being born in Invercargill. Each of us shakes the Director's hand.

We are each given a present, a large bundle wrapped in pink ribbon. There are posters advertising the World Poetry Reading. There is a gold and green cushion, which turns out to contain — or be — a writing pad; there is a Parker pen. There are also several books, mostly about Malay literature, but one turns out to be an anthology of work from the last World Poetry Reading. *Merpati Putih Dan Pelangi/The White Dove and the Rainbow* is 300 pages long, published by the Dewan Bahasa, and has a colour frontispiece showing Kuala Lumpur: 'the city of light and the city of poet'. The poems are all in English and Bahasa Malaysia. The Soviet poet, Bella Akhmadulina, was here last time! Her poems have been translated from Russian into Bahasa Malaysia and thence into English, and have filled with mysterious swerves and wobbles.

October sums up withering.
Nature around is heavy and serious.
In Autumn's late hour — it's so tedious
Again to hurt my elbows against orphanhood's corner.
The neighbour couple's overlong visit
is dragging on and on, and I getting tired with all my soul,
cannot utter a word — in my throat hangs
some sort of deaf-and-dumb vagueness.
In Autumn's late hour — when light is put out
and all of a sudden, when falling asleep, I hearten up with
  the guess
that I was invited to guest
at an artist's place...

From now on, wherever the poets go, presentations will take place. If I remember anything from this week, it will be presentations, flashes of photographic light, little ripples of applause.

Throughout all this Mike Chilton, the NZ High Commissioner, has been sitting on the dais, maintaining an attentive look. Beside him are the Director of Dewan Bahasa and a couple of the organisers of the World Poetry Reading. Now he is allowed to make a speech. It is nicely judged — elegant and brief, and it generates much goodwill, not to mention genial sounds of envy from Thomas Shapcott (who in an earlier incarnation ran the Australian Literature Board and presumably knows a good move when he sees it). There is a handing over of New Zealand poetry and a shaking of hands. But alas the photo opportunities all went to Yugoslavia. The photographers have departed.

Then it is high tea. The High Commissioner detaches himself as fast as decency permits and makes a dash for a waiting limousine. He has to get back to the High Commission, where he is the Chief Returning Officer. They should even have the election results late tomorrow afternoon. Would I like to call round? But tomorrow, along with other poets of the world, I will be in Shah Alam.

DEWAN BAHASA DAN PUSTAKA

The Dewan Bahasa is Malaysia's language and literature agency. It was originally set up as a small government bureau within the old Department of Education. After independence, Malay became an official language of the new nation, and in 1967 the National Language Act made it the sole official language. Back in 1956 the Dewan Bahasa had a staff of sixty. Now a vast office block houses about 1200 people; the Dewan has grown with the language it fosters.

The history of modern Malaysia could be written as a history of the Malay language. In 1969 hundreds were killed in language riots. The Dewan Bahasa is funded by the government to promote a single tongue, Bahasa Malaysia. It plans language campaigns, and it examines and coins the terms that Bahasa Malaysia needs to cope with the specialist terminologies of science, government, technology. In the last thirty years it has compiled and standardised about 600,000 *istilah* or specialised terms. This has made it possible for Malay to become the language of instruction not only in schools but also at university level.

Dewan Bahasa is also a major publisher. As the whole of the Malaysian education system has moved into Bahasa Malaysia, Dewan Bahasa has supplied the textbooks: over 1000 published for schools (many of them translations of English texts); and over the next five years, 800 to be published for university courses. Part of the publishing programme is designed 'to encourage literary and creative growth'. The Dewan runs awards and competitions, workshops and literature forums, and has published about 250 literary titles in the last decade. Some of these are Malay texts translated into other languages (French, English).

Translation can be a problem, however, as Bella Akhmadulina might tell you. Because English is the language of the Raj, it is vigorously discouraged. But it is also the language of trade and international chit-chat — not easily avoided. Because Malaysia has not yet stepped fully clear of the shadow of the Raj, it has hardly become clear to most Malaysians that English is a very, very difficult foreign language. Thus Empire has its mischievous aftermath. Even very weak Malay speakers of English believe their command of the language is wonderfully good. Robert Frost said that poetry is what gets lost in translation; but when Malays translate Malay poetry into English, linguistic competence gets lost: the poets sound inept and silly.

A POETRY SPECTACULAR

Standing room only in the huge auditorium of Kuala Lumpur's City Hall. There are speeches of welcome, and a formal launching of *The White Dove and the Rainbow* by the poet Usman Awang (there is a booklet about him tucked into our conference folder). The international poets loll in the front rows while presentations to dignitaries take place.

Suddenly a man rushes up to me and whispers loudly that I am number four.

'You are France! You read, Mr Bill! You read!'

'No,' I say serenely, 'I am New Zealand.'

'No,' he says. 'You read! Tonight you read! I am warning you!'

I open the programme and point. 'Look, France is there. Number four: France.'

'But France is not here!' he cries. 'France never came to Malaysia. It is you, Mr Bill; when you are called, go quickly!'

I look at the stage with renewed attention. A huge perspex screen hangs at the back. The words *Kuala Lumpur World Poetry Reading* are there, along with the logo of the Dewan Bahasa, while a stylised dove tows the Malaysian flag through a clear sky. Further back, a diorama of clouds streams constantly from left to right. At various points on the stage rainbow banners are strung on wild verticals; white doves hang among them. Suddenly a symphony orchestra pours rich musak through the hall's sound system. Beautiful girls clad all in white leap nimbly about the stage, vaguely courted by men with streamers. For ten minutes they dance — a vision of doves and rainbows. Then the stage is empty.

One by one, we are called — the poet's name and land, and then the poem. One by one we stumble on to the stage. I follow England, Sebastian Barker, whose poem is called 'Thank God Poets Can't Spell'. Because the voice through the loudspeaker says so, I read 'Magasin', a poem about a boy visiting his very sick father, which ends with what must be an impenetrable reference to the second leg at Trentham. Translated into Bahasa Malaysia and declaimed by a very theatrical young woman, it is twice as long as the original and filled with a passion I never knew I was possessed of. The word *Trentham* lingers in the hushed auditorium.

My friend Prayom has a new video camera; he spends the week taking aim around the fringes of events. When I eventually settle exhausted in my seat, he shows me what I look like — swaying among the streamers, muttering nervously as the clouds pour across the sky behind me.

There is theatre in the slow ascent of the elderly Sri Lankan poet, Wimal Abhayasundere, and in his puzzled blinking once he stands in the lights of centre-stage. He begins to sing in a quavering voice. The audience break into spontaneous applause as the first notes sound, then begin to talk loudly through the rest of the poem, 'Conquering Hearts', which is indeed rather long. Wimal reads the English version in a thoroughly prose voice:

The King of Ethina in the gambling arena
Forced in a moment a princess to strip-tease
Out flowed the wailing of the awakening of
the offspring of the earth — the female
Immoralities that prompt the living patterns to go astray
Makes one to abandon good morals
And lays the foundations for commitments of misdeeds...

The talking goes on. Cameras flash. Eventually Wimal finishes. He makes his way down from the stage. His fellow poets rise to take his hand. 'Very interesting,' says Jordan. 'Very interesting, yes,' replies the poet. He is back in his seat by the time the Bahasa Malaysian translation gets underway; he talks animatedly throughout his own translation.

The Chinese poet, Wang Fei-Bai, reads a rhyming poem filled with quotations from Mayakovsky, Lorca, Mallarmé and Matthew Arnold. He wrote his poem in English, so he does it in English first, then in Chinese. 'The world is a watery star/When we behold it from afar.' Turkey reads. Japan reads. Adam Puslojic — a huge beared Yugoslavian who is already one of the characters of the week — reads a poem called 'Breath and Ice'. Afterwards he pauses and cries: 'Little poem for Kuala Lumpur!'

Lord, what age is this one,
when my love is gone?

Adam dashes from the stage, and a moment later tiptoes back to photograph the young woman who is reading the Bahasa Malaysia version of his poem. The auditorium fills with flashlights and applause. The air is dense with the sound of a hundred films automatically rewinding.

Subdued excitement greets the poet from Indonesia. He is famous — a performance reader — and in Malaysia Indonesians are a kind of family. His poem is comic ('naughty', someone tells me later), which may explain why he delivers it like a general declaring war in some terrible movie. But this is poetry as theatre. He strikes poses — left profile, right profile, head tossed back, eyes widening and narrowing with the meaning of his lines — looking for all the world like the front half of a bulldog.

The Romanian poet, Radu Carneci, gives his name, then says the single English sentence he has learnt by heart. 'I am happy to be away from home.'

Thomas Shapcott is the last reader. As he advances towards the stage, the voice cries through the public address system: 'Thomas Shapcott: The Crippled Poet!' But the reference is not to Thomas Shapcott. 'The Crippled Poet' is the name of his poem, which is about a visit to the Malay poet, J.M. Aziz.

At refreshments afterwards, I talk to a distinguished looking man — ex-MP, banker, lawyer and writer of poetry. He has been to Invercargill. We talk about the popularity of poetry in Malaysia. I ask him how well a book of his poems would sell. 'Oh, not well at all. Say 10-15,000 copies.' He asks me why New Zealand never plays any part in the Asia Pacific Film Festival, of which he is one of the organisers. 'We write to them year after year, but no one ever comes.'

27 OCTOBER

Shah Alam is the new capital city of Selangor — some thirty kilometres west of Kuala Lumpur, the federal capital. It is grand and wealthy, still being carved out of the landscape — a confident invention. The state mosque is huge — blues and whites, spires like rocket ships, and its aluminium dome is said to be the largest of its kind in the world.

New Zealand voters are going to the polls as our international poetry coach glides past the mosque. We draw up outside a modern museum. There is a dance of welcome in the foyer; then we file up a staircase to find ourselves in a lecture hall. This is the morning called 'Poets Dialogue'. Poets had been invited to prepare papers on 'The Role of Poetry in a World of Cultural Change' or

'My Creative Experience'. It is not wholly clear who will participate in the dialogue. The programme lists several poets' names, then adds an ominous *etc*. First there are two keynote lectures. Hafiz Arif (aka Harry Aveling, an Australian who is writer in residence at the Dewan Bahasa) gives a brief historical outline of Malay poetry. The Malaysia writer, Baha Zain, delivers a paper called 'Poetry, Poet and Humanity'.

Both men are interested in the question of what is common among cultures and what is culturally distinctive — and what sort of balance needs to be struck between these things. Both clearly believe in belief, and are disturbed, as Harry Aveling puts it, by the common assumption that modern culture is or ought to be secular. Baha Zain refers to Octavio Paz, the latest Nobel prize-winner, as evidence of poetry's importance in public affairs, but the main drive of his speech is against godless ideologies — he attacks several influential but slightly dated Western thinkers: Marx, Freud, Sartre. His paper is a plea for poetry sustained by religious — and especially Islamic — values. 'Poetry was given to us,' he concludes, 'so that we might translate our humanity, and the love of God for all.'

Baha Zain's paper is given in Bahasa Malaysia; but we have a typewritten English translation we can follow. During both papers there has been a sort of continuous muttering from the Soviet quarter. Has Baha Zain offended with his comments on Marx? But no, the Soviet poet has a personal translator, Dr Boris Panikov. Dr Panikov has been giving a running translation into Russian; the whole morning's proceedings are accompanied by a low Cyrillic grumble.

In fact, David Kugultinov — though he looks like a man who has just come from reviewing the troops on Red Square — can hardly be upset by attacks on godless ideologies. He is a Buddhist. And he is a Kalmyk, from Mongolia. He published his first book at eighteen, fought in the Second World War, spent ten years in a detention camp under Stalin. Now he is a people's representative and a member of the Presidium of the Soviet Supreme Council. Occasionally he refers to his friendship with Gorbachev.

He reads his paper in Russian. Boris Panikov translates it into Bahasa Malaysia. Words like *perestroika* occasionally float clear. But we can read the printed English translation. Some of what the poet says sounds interesting. He thinks that language has something to do with poetry. Words vary according to region. Thus the Russian word for sun is hotter than the word used by the Arctic coastal tribe, the Yakut. 'Whereas the word "narn" in my mother tongue of the Kalmyk tribe is hotter than the word "matahari" in the Malay Language, possibly hotter.' Hotter and possibly hotter? It is hard to follow this sort of English. But it is hardly David Kugultinov's fault. His paper is in Russian; it has been put into English by someone whose English wasn't good enough:

> Word is dynamic in its true sense. Allow me to enlighten participants present regarding an invention advocated by a group of scholars of the Institute of Advanced Neural Activities and Neurophysiology in Moscow, headed by an imminent scholar, Paul Simonov. A group of biologists undertook a research on revival of life of a few human who were clinically dead in a ward. The revival was indicated by light impulses emitted from the speech section of the brain projected on the TV. I was astounded by this news. A member of the Ovcinnikov Soviet Academy who passed away recently once told the Soviet people regarding a fact of equal importance. He and his colleagues discovered the human speech gene. Whereas the said gene is not found in the organism of the primetes, such as the gorilla and the chimpanzee or in the organism of the dolphins. As such, it is pointless to attempt to teach animals to talk because only human beings have such ability. This is one of the reasons he rejected the Charles Darwin theory of evolution that human beings are the descendents of the apes. We are the descendents of our parents and our forefathers, and not from the apes. This fact means that the apes that do not possess the speech gene cannot possibly attain the intellectual status of the human being. Although a human possesses the said gene, it can easily deteriorate and be like that of the ape.

This is hard work. Still, as the poet says at the end: 'I feel elated to know that everyone on this earth, be he the follower of Christianity, Islam or Buddhism, whether a capitalist or a communist, can understand our prime need, namely, the preservation of life on our world that is full of beauty and conflict. Long live POETRY!'

Turkey's paper is called 'The Mysterious Sounds Under the Blue Vault (of Heaven)' He has hardly any English but he is determined to read an English translation he has brought with him. The physical agony he goes through is extraordinary — he makes sounds rather than meanings, his voice tightens and knots; each word, each noise, brings a fresh measure of pain:

> The harmonious order of words leads us to poem, the mysterious thing. Poet wraps the skeleton of poem with tulle and produces this pure and great poem. This poem is the harmonious language of poet's inner world henceforth. Perhaps it is the common voice of humanity rising to the blue vault (of heaven). Which language the poet speaks or what nationality he is is not important because all the poets share the same common and universal language. Poet is the person who sees the thing which we cannot see and understands the language of lines, figures and harmony, and then who teaches us this magical language. Poet constructs new musical structures by adding words to his poem. He sends mysterious messages. He travels us on different climates. In fact, poet is the person who searches for the 'absolute' existence and the poems written by him are the mysterious name of this search.
>
> And there are many secrets and treasure under this blue vault and the keys of these are given to the poet's tongue to open them.

Afterwards he collapses into his seat — exhausted by language.

During the week my need for 'correct' English vanishes. Talking will do, saying things which mean things. After a day or two I find I have stopped using the definite article. Deviations from the norm become the norm.

Bahasa Malaysia is interesting. Malaysia is a culture without irony, and I find myself wondering what, as it were, lies behind this absence. It may be a matter of belief. But the language makes many of its plurals by repeating words — *buku buku* is books — and it is hard to be sure that such a language could accommodate irony and survive. Nevertheless, there are some interesting repetitions. Someone tells me that *child child* can sometimes mean adult; and *pig pig*, piggy bank.

The poets come and go. 'Ladies and gentlemen, hello from England,' says Sebastian Barker. The Chinese poet mounts the platform at the start of what is announced as an open question session. He stands at the microphone and tells us about himself. He is not supposed to do this; he is supposed to ask questions, but he has a long paper which he had been expecting to read, 'My Creative Experiences'. He explains that he is a translator and Professor of World Poetry. His pen-name means 'spray of the brine'. He was in a camp during the Cultural Revolution. 'I have good luck to experience life in its vivid variety... Poetry is the best language of understanding...the shortest route between people's hearts.' This is the first time he has left China, the first time he has been able to talk to English speakers in his almost perfect English.

We break for lunch at the Shah Alam Holiday Inn. The lunch is hosted by the Menteri Besar (Chief Minister) of Selangor. There is another poetry reading, and though I am not in the programme I am summoned to read 'Megasin'.

Later we visit the mosque. It is impressive, all right — space, water, tiles and silence. I am most impressed by the shoe racks, and the various prohibitions which deal with dress, with menstruating women.

We look around the museum. There is a wonderful framed enlargement of a photograph showing the Kuala Lumpur flood of 1926. The pith-helmeted men of the British army stand in water up to their waists in the middle of a city street. They face the camera as if nothing unusual is happening.

The museum has several glass cases full of tiny cannons. 'Ho ho, excuse me,' says Dr Boris Panikov. 'Do you know, these cannons, they are small. This is because the Dutch are knowing Malays are very little people.' He chuckles and repeats his joke to all who come along.

The poetry coach takes us into the jungle — a rather Disney-landish jungle called the Malaysian Agriculture Park. This is a 1300 hectare project run by the Agriculture Ministry both as a research and education centre and as a tourist attraction. It is divided into various sections: a padi garden, a spice and beverage garden, a mushroom museum, an animal park, even an 'Idlyllic' Village:

> Come to the Idlyllic Village and the visitor may see for himself the various aspects that make up the ideal homestead Malaysian farmers themselves seek to make their own. Peaceful and laid back, yet vibrant in its make up, this beautiful setting is every farmer's dream of the perfect...

Our destination is the Peak of Fine Arts, a mid-jungle open-air stage on the Greek model. It is the home of the wonderfully named Agro-Theatre, brainchild of the Minister of Agriculture himself. The Agro-Theatre troupe are all full-time employees of the Ministry of Agriculture. 'They are talented and familiar with the vision of the Agricultural policy. In today's presentation, songs, dances and poetry will be rendered in a message-oriented package, depicting the effort of the government and the people of this country to eradicate poverty.'

We watch the performance, along with large bands of schoolchildren who stay on for the international poetry reading which follows. Serbo-Croatian in the manicured jungle. 'Lord, what age is this one/when my love is gone?' I am listed to read on the printed programme, but am not called. One addition to the programme is Maralia Gozo, 'renowned singer and poet from Brazil'. She attended the last World Poetry Reading with her Japanese husband, who was one of the guest poets. (They met at Iowa — where several of the international poets seem to have spent time as students. So America is here after all.) Maralia is a real performer, and has a range of bright costumes which emphasise her body. She puts her mouth around the microphone and makes moaning noises to a backdrop of electronic sound. Before each performance she says: 'Hello, my name is Maralia. I am from Brazil, and I am happy to share my songs with you.' Her first song has a title which seems to be 'Janola'. She is amplified voice and amplified body: total presence. The small Malay men whoop and shriek; their trousers fill with tiny cannons.

Prayom reads today — a poem called 'Missing', which he performs in three absolutely different styles. The first is a sort of prose rendition of the words; the other versions are sung and chanted. Each seems sadder than the last:

I nearly cry at the thought of home.
I've been away because of dismay:
My home disappeared in the fire;
Who will wipe the ashes from my eyes.

Prayom lives in Bangkok, but comes from a provincial village in the north which was burned by Communist insurgents:

'Sweet vegetables, sweet tamarind, white rice,
Beautiful women, virtuous men,'
O the days that sleep forever in the earth,
Is your name dead or alive, o Nakae?

Throughout the performance I watch him, a small figure in black and white, through the viewfinder of his video camera. I am filming Prayom for his family and friends at home, and vaguely aware that his poem is about the impossibility of going home.

At the hotel, he tells me about Thai poetry: the different ways of rendering each poem, the complex systems of rhyme and assonance, cadence and repetition. I always thought skaldic verse must be impossibly difficult to write; but this sounds like the hardest poetry in the world.

We exchange books — and he also gives me a keyring with a tiny Thai cushion attached to it. His wife gave him a plastic bag filled with souvenir keyrings before he left. In my book he writes: 'For Bill, my dear room-mate.'

An evening reading at Central Market. Central Market is in downtown KL. It is rather like London's Covent Garden — an up-market market, a recycled version of a place which was once scruffy, old, real. It is now part of tourist Malaysia; its beautifully preserved exterior houses souvenir stalls, boutiques and restaurants. The poets dismount from their coach and are greeted by a band of small boys doing stylised martial arts.

As we enter the market, young women drape our upper bodies with coloured sashes. We shine in the night, marked out and important, uncomfortably like Miss Universe contestants. We, too, are part of tourist Malaysia. Puzzled shoppers draw back as we promenade among them in our sashes. There is a sprinkling of applause. We pass through a display of our own books and photographs. There is *Zoetropes*. And there is my face beside it: a Robert Cross shot, xeroxed from his book of writers' portraits, faxed through to Kuala Lumpur, then xeroxed once again. Most of the international poets just look ten years younger, but I have dissolved and drifted and am hardly there at all.

The display includes sample verses. Some of the English versions have interesting moments, like this one from a poem by Germany:

The method of abroad
just brought me strepafaction
— not the inner freedom

We leave the market by another door and find ourselves at a small sound-shell on the riverbank. We sit, distinctive in our poetry sashes, while Malay and Chinese children perform traditional dances. Lizards scuttle up and down the stage backdrop. It is cute and multicultural. A small Tamil girl reads a poem she has written for the international poets:

Malaysia is a lovely land
Everyone will lend a helping hand
The food is quite massive
Everything is here to receive

The poets read. Children crowd around asking for autographs.

This must be how the All Blacks feel. My pen knocks against something metallic on my sash. It is a badge with a cheerful monkey on it. 'Central Market!' says the monkey. 'Visit Malaysia Year 1990.'

28 OCTOBER

Today we are travelling to the state of Negeri Sembilan. Meantime the morning paper carries the New Zealand election results. *Annihilated* is the word used to describe what has happened to Labour.

There are two coaches, one loaded with international poets, the other with local poets. For a moment we stop by a cemetery. It is a Christian graveyard full of Second World War dead. The large flat field contains many small unmarked stones, like distance markers on a roadway. A car is parked beside one grave. A middle-aged Chinese couple have placed six candles on the slab. They light them and stand still a moment. Then they get in the car and drive across the grass to another grave where they light more candles. They come back to check the first grave. The flames seem to sputter out in the breeze, then spring back to life like trick candles from a joke shop. Now the couple get in their car and drive away.

Negeri Sembilan is south of Selangor. After we cross the state boundary, we stop at a cultural complex, whose main building — though it now houses an exhibition of traditional costumes — was originally constructed as the pavilion for the 1984 International Koran Reading Competition. There is dance and music, some menhirs which I photograph, buildings whose rooflines follow the Minangkabau style said to be based on buffalo horns. Each of the poets is presented with a hardboiled egg attached to a paper flower.

The coaches move on. Something must be wrong: the sound of wailing sirens can be heard. But we have been picked up by a police escort — sirens proclaim us as we go, red lights flash. Throughout the day all other traffic pulls over to the side of the road as our poetry motorcade zooms by. We visit a Sultan's palace. Lunch is a banquet with the Chief Minister of Selangor — a diminutive version of David Lange who makes a long, witty, wholly impromptu speech in Bahasa Malaysia which none of the poets understand. The Malaysians roar with laughter. The Chief Minister presents us each with a specially-inscribed lacquered coconut shell. We present him with framed posters promoting the World Poetry Reading. Back on the bus, someone explains that the video team which dogs us everywhere we go is making a permanent record of the week for Dewan Bahasa. We can order copies: US$10.00.

Much later in the day — after the motorcade has passed through rustic scenery and undulating hills, rubber plantations and palm oil groves — we arrive in the grounds of a pseudo-Tudor guest-house, a seaside retreat which dates from the days of the Raj. We can eat here, swim if we like. There is an abandoned summer-house on an island at the end of the pier. It is hot and steamy — vaguely vandalised. Some of the Muslim poets go out to the island and pray.

It is not quite clear who is who; but we are meeting with some of the writers of Negeri Sembilan, the local PEN branch. There is a banquet under marquees; and an impromptu poetry reading through a portable sound system. Norway reads. Switzerland reads. Then there is an interruption. A furious man yells at the compere. The poetry reading has gone on too long; it is preventing people from observing evening prayers. 'So we will be stopped,' says the compere, 'for our ten minutes or so for those of the prayerful to have a wash and say their prayers, and then our readings will continue.'

The readings never resume, and eventually we are taken by coach, a ten-minute ride through the dark, to Port Dickson's Festival arena. We descend into a giant amusement park. There are lights and crowds of people — sideshows, merry-go-rounds, ferris wheels. The poets are the evening concert's highlight. Seasoned troupers by now, we cheer each other and strut our stuff. I read 'Zoetropes' through a sound system which easily drowns out the chattering teenagers drifting by, the girls screaming from the nearby Horror House, the motorbikes which roar around the Wall of Death.

29 OCTOBER: DISCUSSION ON WORLD CONTEMPORARY ISSUES

In the hotel lobby poets sign each other's programmes. 'Thank you,' says Sri Lanka, 'it is for my history.' Jordan writes a message in every programme: 'Hello! Be happy, unhappy, be whatever you want. You are a poet.' Someone says that yesterday's lunch-time readings were on television.

Today we visit the Dewan Bahasa. We are greeted by the Director, who makes a speech. We watch a split-screen audiovisual display about the Dewan and applaud when it ends. 'Multi-vision show' says the programme. We ascend by lift to the top of the building where we find ourselves in a great council room with a horseshoe-shaped seating plan. The room is full of flags and portable shrubs; there is an expensive parquet floor. It looks like one of those chambers where international conferences take place. But then, we *are* an international conference: we even sit behind individual microphones. This must be the 'Discussion on World Contemporary Issues'.

The moderator tells us that this is meant to be informal. 'Any topic under the sun except poetry'. He beams.

The international poets who happen to be women have been waiting for a forum like this one. Each of them wants to ask the same question. In the event it is Mousse Boulanger from Switzerland who speaks.

'I wonder if the Malaysian poets here, women or men, will say something about the position of women in this country? Some of us are a little puzzled about it, you see.'

The moderator sits a little straighter. 'All is equal in Malaysia,' he says. 'But let me say, Islam, well, we should have a separate section where we will discuss this. But put aside this question for the mean time, I thank you.'

Black clouds have been gathering at the windows; now the moderator's words are accompanied by rolling thunder. Rain rattles on the roof above our heads.

A long silence produces a more specific question. The questioner is an elegant, middle-aged Japanese woman, with short blue hair. Where has she come from? She wishes to know about polygamy. Is it a Malaysian matter or an Islamic matter? A Malaysian woman at one end of the horseshoe raises her hand — she would like to make a reply, or add a comment. The chair ignores her, looking anxiously around the room. Kemala comes to the rescue.

'In Malaysia, unlike Islam, men have to have first wife's permission before taking another wife. So this is very different from Islam. But actually women are very privileged in our society. It is great privilege here for women. They are not inferior, they are not even equal, no, in Malaysia they are privileged indeed.'

The Western women look astonished. But now a poet from the Middle East is on his feet, quaking with fury. 'These matters,' he says, 'they are entirely accidental. I know people who sometimes have three wives. For example, the first wife is a cousin who gets no husband and because he is good to his family he has her out of pity. Yes pity. This is goodness, you see, absolute goodness.' His voice gets louder as he goes on. 'So there was a second wife. *Of course there would be.* So now the second wife, she gets handicapped. And there is the third wife therefore. This is how such things happen. And so I say to you: *Don't you compare cultures*! There are things we do not like in your culture. But do I say them? So this is not a great issue, I think. Three wives, and it is all fine. This is cultures and how they work. The world is a place of conscience and judgement and these are all for us to show. Now let us get rid of this issue and go to other things.'

But the astonished room cannot get rid of the issue. The Malaysian woman — a Tamil, I realise — still has her hand up. There is a sort of smile on her face; she knows she will never get the nod from the chair. Some of the Western men have decided to be peacemakers. Dr Boris Panikov rises.

'I am wishing to warn the women gathered here of the dangers of revolution. Progress, yes. But revolution, it is very dangerous. Very dangerous indeed. I am from Soviet Union, as you know. We know revolution. Oh how we know revolution. So abstain from revolution if you can. This is what I have to say to you women of the world. Thank you.'

He sits but the thunder and the rain go on. People glance around the unlucky horsehoe. Mousse Boulanger decides to defuse things herself. She shifts discussion to the political structure of Malaysia. How many states are there in Malaysia? How do central and district governments work together and divide responsibilities?

At this point a chair is pushed back on my left, and Merlinda C. Bobis (Philippines) walks from the room. She has had enough. On my right Anne Szumigalski (Canada) has made a page-size doodle on her pad — a giant tree-like woman totters on spindly shoes; her body flaps and flows, giving birth to a hundred faces.

Sebastian Barker asks a question. 'I wonder what is the writer's responsibility to the United Nations and to individual politicians? What is the writer's role really?' Silence. 'What do you think?' says the moderator. 'Oh. What do I think? Well I'm just asking the question to get the discussion going again. But if you really want to know, I think we need to talk to individual politicians when we meet them. This is what poets everywhere must do.'

Anne Szumigalski throws down her doodle and begins to speak into her microphone. Around the horseshoe men look anxious. Then there is a deafening crash from the sky — the lights go out, our microphones go dead, the thunder rolls.

30 OCTOBER

Prayom departs; we photograph each other and shake hands. The Norwegians and Sebastian Barker are off to Bangkok, too. I find Chinatown's Petaling Street and buy fake designer gear — hammering the prices down by about 25 per cent, feeling pleased in the way that only someone who knows he has not really bargained at all feels pleased.

The formalities of the week are over. No more readings. But in the afternoon we are on the coach again. Some poets whisper that the furious Middle Eastern poet had been describing himself. He currently has two wives — each in a different country. Who knows? We find ourselves at the National University. Malay nationalism and Islam are serious on this campus, hard to separate one from the other. Most female students are fully covered, and peer through pillarbox eye openings. The University is devoted to Malay culture, we are told, and is mostly a research institute — no undergraduate students.

We meet the Director of the Institute of Malay Culture, who makes a small speech about Bahasa Malaysia and gives us a book of his own, a collection of polemical pieces on nationalist and ethnic matters.

The international poets take turns reading poems to one another around the table. This impromptu session is the most enjoyable and useful reading of all: something to do with poetry and cultural exchange begins to happen. Our host, the director, listens for a few minutes — then makes his way to an adjoining room where, fully visible and audible through a glass wall, he engages in animated conversation with a colleague.

The final event, the final evening. We are to dine at the house of the poet, Usman Awang. We have been told that it will be possible to drink alcohol this evening: the age of orange cordial is over. The coach will make a special stop at a bottle store. The international poets, led by the Eastern Europeans, descend on the bottle store. I buy half-a-dozen cans of Tiger lager. The Pakistani poet buys two large bottles of codliver oil — for some reason sales of codliver oil are prohibited in Pakistan. He is happy: already he can see his family rejoicing, running to meet him from the plane.

When we get to Usman Awang's, we are told to leave our purchases on the bus; we may be able to fetch them later — but first someone must ascertain that it is really all right. Usman Awang has a large, elegant residence. There are tables on a patio, a small band, many people milling about, stumbling over the roaming video crew. I find myself at a table next to a man who introduces himself as the Prime Minister's Secretary. Ann Szumigalski is at the table; also Merlinda C. Bobis from the Philippines, Tom Shapcott, and a young North American who teaches law at a local university. We eat and discuss Malaysian fruit — its variety, its abundance.

'And yet the oddest thing,' says the young lawyer, 'I bought some bananas the other day which came from the Philippines.'

'Excuse me,' says the Prime Minister's Secretary, addressing the table generally, 'excuse me but I must tell you that this is untrue.'

'Oh it's true,' says the lawyer, sipping his orange cordial. 'I saw the little stickers on them: "Produce of the Philippines".'

'We do grow a lot of bananas in the Philippines,' says Merlinda.

'No, no, no, this is impossible! Malaysia does not import bananas, it exports them!'

'But I had to peel the little stickers off.'

'You are wrong! You are wrong! I declare that you are wrong!' The Prime Minister's Secretary will brook no further argument. He rises and leaves the table.

Word is passed around that we may fetch our alcohol. But rain is pouring, and the coach is parked a block away. Anyway, now a microphone has appeared and guests and hosts sing songs. The Malays sing pantoums, which turn out to be lively improvisational choral pieces; the international poets sing their national songs. I grind through a rousing version of 'Tutira mai', and when the party is about to break up and our hosts are half-heartedly humming 'Auld Lang Syne' to an insecure guitar — at a loss both for words and for melody — I find myself seized by a strange desire to assert whatever cultural heritage I have. Swept forward on the tide of my own foolishness, I seize the microphone and lead the assembled poets in several rounds of 'Auld Lang Syne'. Tom Shapcott is pushed forward to join me, and together we drift around the text. I am beginning to enjoy this — perhaps I could go on to 'Now is the Hour'? Or 'Ten Guitars'? 'You are My Sunshine'? — no trouble, just let me get organised here, whatever does Usman Awang put in his orange cordial? — but in fact we seem to be on the bus again, groaning through the night towards the Holiday Inn, downtown Kuala Lumpur, where as I climb into my own wee bed it occurs to me that all of this will be on the official video.

31 OCTOBER

People are leaving today. Many of the poets have cards and exchange them. Sri Lanka's card says:

Pandit Wimal Abhayasundere:
Poet, Writer, Lyricist.

Turkey has a printed card which says: *Mehmed Atilla Maras — Engineer*. Underneath he has written in blue ink: *poet*.

At breakfast Merlinda C. Bobis talks about the Russians. After the scene at the Dewan Bahasa, David Kugultinov, foe of Stalin and comrade of Gorbachev, explained to her, through his interpreter, Dr Boris Panikov, that such a beautiful girl as she should be having babies, not writing poems. In fact, he explained, it is a well known fact that to men falls the task of making beautiful poems. It is hard work, man's work. Merlinda does not need to write poems; she can simply look beautiful; she *is* a poem.

McPIMP

I go shopping and come across the Kuala Lumpur McDonald's, where I order a shake and a McRendan, a spiced Malaysian burger. I meet my first dubious fellow, who lurks nearby, then slips across and asks about my shake. 'Is icecream in there? How you like Kuala Lumpur? How long you here?' When he discovers I've been here a week and am leaving later today, his face drops, he slides away. I tuck into my McRendan.

Then my friend is back, he sits and gives me his name. I give him mine, and he calls me Mr Bill.

'You would like my sister, Mr Bill. She is going to your country.

New Zealand isn't it? She will study, you can come to our house and tell her all these things. She will be grateful.'

The circumstances of his story grow more elaborate as he goes along. He names the city she will go to — 'Where you from? Wellington? Well, amazing! This is where she is going, Mr Bill, she will be please to see you.' — and throws in a sick mother, whom his sister nurses. He himself is in the import/export business. If only I were staying longer, he would take me to see his sister, I could give her advice, and she is very friendly, very *loving*.

'Do you have time for today perhaps Mr Bill? A quick visit to my sister?'

No, I say, I must catch my aeroplane and before that I must buy gifts for my wife and children. Can my friend suggest any good places to shop?

'Oh, anywhere at all. Well, very nice to see you.' He shakes my hand and is gone.

I have hardly seen Malaysia. Air-conditioned coaches, international hotels, lecture halls. But the country is an economic prodigy. Last year the state of Johore created 130,000 jobs and is anxious about how it can fill the 250,000 new job vacancies which are projected in the next decade. The country as a whole expects a 10 per cent growth rate during 1991. I have met something of the Malaysia that is trying to create the culture to match the economic growth. The government has made huge investments in culture and education; even its combining of the Tourism and Culture portfolios in a single ministry seems obviously sensible.

When I get back home, I will learn that New Zealand's new Minister of Tourism is John Banks, who is also the Minister of Police.

The Kuala Lumpur World Poetry Reading has very little to do with world poetry. But it is not just an item on the Malaysian tourist calendar. It is mostly about Malay nationalism and self-esteem; a small part of the process by which Malay culture is being transformed into Malaysian culture. Bahasa Malaya is now called Bahasa Malaysia: it is to be the language of all the people of the nation. As for the world, its languages and poets are here as part of that nation-building exercise: our job is to dignify the *single* language, the *single* culture, of our hosts. Of course one or two of us, as usual, are learning the extent of our own ignorance.

The Malays are quiet, watchful, generous people. Anxiety and hospitality are equally matched in many of those I meet. In that sense it is just like being at home. The Prime Minister's Secretary's preoccupation with bananas is simply one way in which anxiety surfaces. Throughout the week people ask me if the Fan Club — a New Zealand pop group which has (I think) a Malay singer — is as much admired in New Zealand as in Malaysia. Since I have never heard of the Fan Club, my answers are rather evasive, and the watchful faces grow even more watchful.

On the day I leave Malaysia it is announced that the price of soft drinks is going up. The Australian and New Zealand Graduates Association of Malaysia is gathering for a talk on air-conditioning systems by engineer Paul Lau. At the Sapphire Discotheque there will be an attractive gift for the Most Outrageous Halloween guest. My horoscope says: 'You have nowhere to go today but back to the beginning — and where is that? You'll know before the day is out.'

KOALA LUMPUR

Yesterday Malaysia Airlines — which has just taken on twenty ex-Air New Zealand pilots — made its inaugural flight to Vienna. They imported the Vienna Ladies Orchestra to mark the occasion. The Vienna Ladies Orchestra is a remarkable combo — it can split into three groups to perform in three different countries simultaneously.

And today it is Malaysia Airlines' inaugural flight to Brisbane. My journey home will be via Australia. Glamorous hostesses prowl about the departure lounge, distributing tiny koalas and promotional brochures for the Gold Coast. High above us a large television screen is filled with skyscrapers and ocean, the joys of Surfers.

A giant koala bear is waddling about the lounge. It poses with Japanese tourists for photographs. It snuggles up to a pair of puzzled body builders. Small Malay children scream and burst into tears. The koala bear advances mercilessly through the room, flanked by airline staff, holding out its hand to everyone it passes.

'Giddy might!' says a high-pitched Asian voice.

I look up. The koala bear is standing beside me. 'Giddy might!' says the tiny voice from deep inside the costume. It holds out its paw.

At this very moment — it is exactly 7 p.m. — the voice of the muezzin summoning the faithful to prayer calls from the airport public address system. Above us the television screen fills with the domes and spires of Islam.

I look back at the koala. 'Giddy might,' it says.

'Gidday,' I say, and reach to take its hand.

The Brain of Katherine Mansfield

1

You are just an ordinary New Zealander. You have strength, intelligence and luck, though you are not particularly good at languages. Your family and friends like you, and there is one special friend who really thinks you're swell. Yours is a well-rounded personality; your horoscope is usually good; your school report says 'satisfactory'. But somehow you are restless. Your life is missing challenge and excitement. You want to make things happen. Go to 2.

2

On your way home from school one day, you find an old man waiting outside your house. He is holding a leather-bound book. He looks as if he has been expecting you.

'I have been reading your story,' he says. 'But it seems to have stopped. Something seems to happen when you enter the house.'

He goes on to explain that he is eager to know how your life will continue. In fact, he says, your life is essentially an unwritten story. You yourself are the hero of the story.

'Many are the choices you must face, but the outcome of the tale will depend on you alone.'

You stare at the stranger speechless, but your heart is beating with excitement. Dimly, as at a distance, you hear him say that you will need more than human help on the adventures which await you: you must choose one of three magic weapons to take with you on your journey. But you will have to come with him to his house. It lies in a distant suburb of the city.

It is getting late. The dark clouds of a winter afternoon swoop down over the familiar hills and houses. You shiver. The time of your first decision is upon you. Do you dare to turn the pages of adventure?

If you decide to accompany the old man, go to 5.
If you decide to go home and think it over, go to 11.

3

You wrestle with the helicopter's controls as the machine spirals helplessly down towards the jagged ridges of one of New Zealand's premier National Parks. Your resourcefulness is in vain. All of a sudden the helicopter motor cuts out and you are plunging through the thick carpet of bush which... But everything goes black.

Go to 24.

4

Your plane circles over Christchurch. It banks over Cathedral Square. You suck contentedly on your sweet. In the distance you can see the snow-clad Southern Alps, like a distant promise of adventures yet to come.

Suddenly the captain's voice crackles over the intercom. There has been a bomb threat, responsibility as yet unclaimed. 'Assume crash positions! Assume crash positions!' All around you passengers are screaming. A few place their heads between their knees, some embrace loved ones. But it is all beside the point. If you have the Jump Thermos with you, drink quickly and go to 15. Otherwise, grit your teeth. The plane is about to explode into a thousand pieces.

This is an early end to your adventure, but you may like to console yourself with the thought that this disaster will almost certainly be the lead news item in bulletins throughout the world. Think of Erebus. Think of Mr Asia. Close the book.

5

You are in the old man's front room. It is dimly lit, a candle flickers, and from another part of the house there is the noise of a radio: the night trots from Forbury. On a sideboard there are three strange objects, each glowing with a faint light. A piece of greenstone. An orange thermos. A small red pocket knife.

The old man explains. The first object is called a 'Pounamu Decoder'. It enables you to understand the words of any living creature, even the secret languages of animals and birds. It is essentially, he says, a translation facility.

The orange thermos contains a secret potion. If you are in a place of danger and you drink from it, you will be instantly transported elsewhere. It is a 'Jump Thermos'.

The knife is a 'Swiss Army Knife'. It is a powerful weapon which will destroy in battle any person or creature foolhardy enough to attack you. It has magical properties conferred on it by the gnomes who forged it so many centuries ago. (Note: ineffective against the bowmen of the emperor or the Dark Lord of Kwesta-kaa.) It also has scissors and a toothpick.

You may choose only one of these magic weapons. You must decide now. Do you choose the Pounamu Decoder? the Jump Thermos? the Swiss Army Knife?

When you have made your choice, proceed to 6.

6

The old man motions you to sit down. He tells you that you have chosen wisely. He begins to read from the leather-bound book.

'You are just an ordinary New Zealander,' he says. 'You have a well-rounded personality, you collect stamps and are reasonably good at sport. You and your folks go camping in the summer. But somehow you are restless. You were not born for routine pleasures. You decide to see something of your country. You make your way to the airport and within minutes you are airborne...'

If you wish to disembark at Christchurch airport, go to 4.
If you would rather go to Invercargill, try 15.

7

You are whisked off on a magic carpet ride across the fiords and mountains of New Zealand's southern wonderland. Sometimes the copter soars effortlessly above razor-sharp peaks, sometimes it darts through a narrow gorge, brushing the sides of spectacular mountain walls, giving you chance after chance to snap the magnificent vistas which open up on all sides. Here Nature outdoes herself effortlessly. Whoops! mind that rock wall! Let's hope no one was in the path of that avalanche! Yes, flight of a lifetime. Rugged splendour. Mitre Peak. Wild blue yonder. Sutherland Falls.

But what has happened? The helicopter pilot has leant out too far. Oh no! He has fallen from the machine, he hurtles and corkscrews down until he lies, a broken matchstick figure, on the rocks below.

No one has ever taught you how to operate a helicopter. A sip of the Jump Thermos, if you have it, will take you to 22. Otherwise you can seize the controls and do what you can — in which case go to 3. Or you can close your eyes and hope for the best — go to 14.

8

You do not need a Pounamu Decoder to understand *this* speech! It soon becomes clear that Rebecca plans to keep you as her mate. Admittedly she is really rather attractive... But you have a girl back home. With a superhuman effort you break free from your bonds!

If you have the Jump Thermos, you quickly reach for it and put it to your lips. Too late! Rebecca dashes it from your hands. The precious potion soaks into the earth. Go to 9.

9

Rebecca overpowers you once more. You must submit to your fate. Rebecca keeps you for her pleasure but, in the way of things, she tires of you after three or four days and drops you at the side of the road somewhere between Milton and Balclutha. Nine months later she will bear a child, a boy whom she gives the name Hank Mushroom. He will grow up to be New Zealand's finest Country & Western singer. His most famous song will be 'Cowboy Clothes', the one with that catchy chorus:

I think I was in love with you
But you know that feelin' goes.
Still I'll try to get to like you
In your cowboy clothes.

This can mean nothing to you, however, for you are about to be run down and killed by a passing sheep-truck as you hobble along the median strip in the direction of Balclutha. Close the book.

10

You rub the Pounamu Decoder. A mist comes before your eyes and for a moment you can see nothing. You are in that dark place between one language and another where so many things go wrong. But slowly you begin to make out Wairarapa's words:

> Fashion well your daughter's legs,
> That she may look well by the beach-fire.
> If I must die, let me die on my land.
> Deep in throat, shallow in muscles.
> It's evening that breaks the spade.

His old voice begins to falter. But he draws in breath and continues:

> Make the most of your time while you are young.
> A flounder would not go back to the mud it has stirred.
> There's a sea that breaks.
> There's a sea that doesn't.

Well, this is certainly not the Wairarapa of old. Can this really be the plucky old soldier who was once caretaker at Ferndale District High? You wish him good fortune on his quest and journey on your way. You do not look back, but you are sure that the grief-stricken old fellow keeps on waving long after you have rounded a bend and have vanished from sight. Go to 12.

11

Fool! Miserable worm! Prepare to pay the price of your despicable need for security. You enter the house to find the bloody bodies of your parents on the floor. Also your puppy, Shane. Even now an escaped axe murderer lies in wait for you behind the bathroom door. The adventure on which you refused to embark is already over. Close the book.

12

You continue along the road, occasionally trying to thumb down a car. But nothing stops. A cheeky fantail begins to follow you. He dips and swerves above you, coming close, then darting out of reach. He chirps and chirps. It is as if he is trying to tell you something.

Wait a minute! Do you have the Pounamu Decoder? If you do, go to 42 and learn the meaning of the fantail's song. If you possess some other weapon, bad luck. Go to 25 and continue to try your luck at hitch-hiking.

13

Here is what Rebecca says:

> Hey hey hey, this is supposed to be fun, not drudgery. If you're at an impasse, the odds are that you're not having fun. Run around the block. Fix yourself a drink. Chop wood. Flip through one of my many sex manuals. Get away and come back.
>
> If you have tried making changes and still find yourself immobilised, then it may be time to look at your attitude towards the whole project. The stickiest attitude, the one which causes creative people like you the most grief is…
>
> What's your answer?
>
> Your answer is the right answer for you. Hey hey hey.
>
> It is the one you have to tackle.

Rebecca continues in this vein for many hours. Your brain throbs with pain. If only you had chosen the Jump Thermos. You make a superhuman effort, burst free of your bonds and… staggering Minerva! your very wish has been strong enough to effect physical portation! You feel the molecules of your body dissolving. They reassemble at 36.

14

You close your eyes. Suddenly the helicopter seems to be gripped by an invisible hand. You feel yourself being lifted through the air, and before you have time to work out what is happening, you find yourself in a circular room made of some strange metal material as yet unknown to humankind. Slowly the true nature of your situation dawns on you. You are in an alien spacecraft, in orbit around the Earth. You guess, too, that this explanation has been somehow implanted in your brain. You feel fingers combing through the inside of your head. Fiends! Why will they not show themselves and communicate like normal human beings?

Suddenly a figure robed in white materialises before you. He raises a hand and you feel the fury within you quelled. He speaks to you, making strange sing-song sounds which you cannot understand. If you have the Pounamu Decoder, go to 40, where you will find a translation of the alien being's incomprehensible noises.

If you have the Swiss Army Knife and think it may be possible to overcome the alien and take control of the spaceship, go to 32, where you may mount your attack.

15

Hooray! You land safely at Invercargill. The tarmac shines, for a light rain is falling. You shiver. The evening is chill; you are far from family and friends. All the same, you can be assured of a genuine southern welcome. Now you must transfer to your hotel for overnight accommodation. Go to 18.

16

It's a nice day here.
Very quiet and warm.
Even the milkman crying milk
sounds to me like a bird
trying its note.

I shall tell everything.
The moon is rising
and in the sky
there's a flying yellow light
like the wings of canaries.

Hey hey hey.

The bird repeats the song over and over, each time looking a little more pleased with itself. Has it not *heard* of the death of the author? Whether or not you feel this translation has helped you, proceed to 45.

17

You cautiously approach. Can it be? Is it? Yes. No. Yes! it is Wairarapa, he whom you knew in former days. Does he recognise you? His face is twisted in pain. He must be searching still for his lost daughter, the one who set off to hitch-hike around the South Island and was never seen again. There was that big fuss on television. It was in all the papers, you remember. He is as calm and reassuring as ever, yet somehow inscrutable. But what is he trying to tell you?

Ah, Wairarapa is addressing you in Maori. There is urgency in his voice. He grips your arm. Noble old man, does he not understand that you do not know the Maori tongue? Tahi rua toru wha. Why does he go on like this? Has he been radicalised or something?

> Toia nga waewae o to tamahine,
> Kia tau ai te tu i te ahi taipari.
> Kia mate au, mate ki te kainga.
> Hohonu kaki, papaku uaua.
> He ahiahi whatiwhati kaheru.
>
> Mahia nga mahi kei tamariki ana.
> E kore te patiki e hoki ano ki tona puehu.
> Tena te ngaru whati.
> Tena te ngaru puku.

If you are carrying the Pounamu Decoder, go to 10. If not, there is evidently nothing to be done. But this is certainly no longer the plucky war veteran who was once caretaker at Ferndale District High. He must be crazed with grief at the loss of his daughter. 'Farewell, e koro,' you say, and continue on your way. Go to 12.

18

A restful night's sleep and you are free to sightsee at your leisure. Why not take a trip out to Oreti Beach, or stroll in the sunken rose gardens at Queens Park? Find time, too, to look at the Museum, opposite the part entrance, outside which you can see the statue of Minerva, Roman Goddess of Wisdom.

'Lend me your wisdom, oh Goddess,' you whisper, as you anticipate the ordeals which lie ahead.

But now it is time for your experience of a lifetime. Go at once to 7.

19

You enter the cave cautiously. It is damp and dark. You edge your way into the heart of the mountain, feeling with your hands along the rough rock wall. You think you hear a cough. Before you can turn, someone — or something — strikes you a hard blow on your head. You slump to the cavern floor. You feel rough hands seize you.

A voice mutters: 'Yes, this is the one. Bear him to the master.'

But this is the last thing you remember. Everything goes black. Proceed to 46.

20

The track soon peters out. Maybe this was a bad decision. You push your way through the dense undergrowth, and feel that dark eyes watch you as you go. This is a patient, brooding landscape. It is as if something is waiting, who knows for what. It is as if the waiting began long before you were born.

Suddenly you spy a curious white powder at the foot of a majestic totara tree. Perhaps it is the magic potion which Douglas the Elf told you of?

If you decide to investigate further, go to 33.

If you prefer to continue on your way, go to 47.

21

Something — or someone — strikes you a hard blow on the back of your skull. You slump to the floor and pass into a bewildering world of darkness and swirling colours. When you wake you are at 31.

22

A place of darkness. Mist and shafts of light. As in a dream you see:

a band of boisterous dwarves; the bowmen of the emperor; a phantom haka party; Mr Brathwaite who used to be your teacher in Standard Two at Dipton Primary School; roaming elves and orcs.

You feel confused. Take a further draught from the Jump Thermos and go to 27.

23

You walk till night falls. You realise you must keep going. To pause now might prove fatal. In eerie moonlight you make your way between the towering walls of rocky gorges. You skirt giant stones around which the furious water snarls and roars. This is Nature's playground. Perhaps you, too, are merely a toy of the gods? A cloud, small, serene, floats across the moon.

Great Minerva, you whisper inwardly, if ever I needed help of thine then the hour is surely come.

Suddenly, off to your left, you see a clearing. There are lights, and figures moving.

If you decide to investigate, go to 35.

If you feel it would be better to wait till dawn and seek overnight shelter in a nearby cave, go to 19.

24

A place of darkness. Mist and shafts of light. As in a dream you see:

tattooed warriors; the bowmen of the emperor; the last Moriori; a team of Lands and Survey workers; anxious possums; gnomes walking in a circle.

Go to 44.

25

Just when you begin to despair of ever getting a lift, a large sheep-truck pulls up. The driver is an amiable sort of fellow. He asks you where you are going, and tells you that he is heading for Owaka, today being the day of Owaka's annual rodeo. Would that be any use to you?

You are barely able to conceal your excitement. 'Would it *what*!' you say.

You make desultory conversation with the truckdriver as the countryside speeds by. After a time you have a craving for a cigarette. You are just about to light up, when you wonder if you ought to ask the truckdriver's permission.

If you ask the truckdriver's permission, go to 34.
If you decide to light up anyway, go to 28.

26

You see three doors. They are identical, except for the names above them. Over the door on the left it says, 'The Portal of the Past'. Over the middle door it says, 'The Portal of Ingestion'. Over the door on the right it says, 'The Portal of Other Possibilities'.

The figure in white indicates that you are to choose one of these doors, and go through it. The doors slowly slide open. You crane your neck but beyond each door you can see only stars and the infinite darkness of the universe. You step uncertainly towards the door of your choosing…

If you choose the Portal of the Past, go to 43.
If you choose the Portal of Ingestion, go to 49.
If you choose the Portal of Other Possibilities, go to 24.

27

A place of darkness. Mist and shafts of light. As in a dream you see:

the Mayor of Balclutha; the Howard Morrison Quartet; the bowmen of the emperor; sealers and whalers at their trades; the string section of the New Zealand Symphony Orchestra; Rebecca the mushroom farmer.

You peer inside the Jump Thermos. Just enough for one last sip. But then the flask will be empty.

If you drink from the Jump Thermos, go to 36.
If you decide to wait and see what happens, go to 21.

28

You inhale a lungful or two of smoke. You exhale. The smoke fills the cab.

The truckdriver's fury has to be seen to be believed. If there is one thing he hates more than smoking, he says, it is your sort of rudeness. He flings open the door and throws you from the moving cab. Your bloody body rolls into a ditch, where — after a few hours — you die. Maybe Wairarapa will find you and give you decent burial. But maybe he has covered this stretch of road already? Close the book.

29

In a swift jack-knifing movement you launch yourself at Herr Schneidermann, simultaneously flicking open the Swiss Army Knife. A look of fear crosses your opponent's face, only to be replaced by one of triumph. For you are attacking him with the toothpick.

The struggle is brief and one-sided. Herr Schneidermann seems to be gifted with superhuman strength, and in one hand he wields a surgical scalpel. In a few moments he has subdued you. Once more you find yourself bound on the operating table, but this time you are bleeding profusely.

Herr Schneidermann gazes disdainfully down at you. He opens the Swiss Army Knife.

'Foolish boy. I shall use your amusing instrument to remove your brain. Your body is now too damaged to be of use to me.'

He asks your name, and you name yourself with pride. He checks the spelling with you, then writes it on the label of a glass jar. Soon you will lose consciousness. For you, this story is over. But maybe your brain will live on in the body of some future adventurer. Until then it must wait in a jar between Minnie Dean and the legendary Colin Meads. Close the book.

30

You continue to follow the creek downstream. Sometimes you trip over stones, or slip on the wet clay banks. You clutch at ferns to stop yourself falling. Always you are accompanied by the insistent warning cries of birds.

From time to time other creeks tumble into the muddy channel you are following. They hail each other as old friends do, and the banks widen to accommodate the newcomers. In one place you stop to admire a slender waterfall. You could almost swear you see movement—a man? a large animal?—behind the dazzling spray. Should you investigate? It may be nothing. On the other hand, it may be dangerous. Perhaps best to continue on your way.

If you decide to investigate the cave behind the waterfall, go to 19.
If you press on along the creek, go to 23.

31

Slowly you return to consciousness. Your head aches. You realise that you have been bound and gagged, and that you are in a derelict goldminer's cottage somewhere in Central Otago. You have been captured by Rebecca the mushroom farmer.

Rebecca the mushroom farmer enters the room and stares at you with undisguised interest. She tells you at length about the Home Science degree she is doing extramurally from the University of Otago. She describes the personal computer she is going to get in order to make stock management more viable. But it is strange, Rebecca seems to speak as if she operated by remote control. Her speech grows slurred; it becomes slower and slower and starts to sound like another language. You cannot understand her.

If you have the Pounamu Decoder and wish to know what she is saying, go to 13. If not, go to 8.

You may not use the Swiss Army Knife, assuming you are carrying it. It would be unsporting to use such a weapon against a woman.

32

You are brave but foolhardy. With one swift move you slip the Swiss Army Knife from your trouser pocket, flick it open and launch yourself at the creature in white. But you have pulled out the wrong blade! You are attacking him with the bottle opener. Before you know it, you are lifeless, a corpse doomed to float forever through the dark reaches of space. Bad luck, but there you are. Or more precisely, there you aren't. Better luck some other time. Close the book.

33

You wet your finger and dip it in the white powdery substance. Then you lick your finger. A curious taste, it seems to burn your tongue. Fool! This is cyanide poison, which trappers have laid for possums. You will be dead within a minute. As your life passes before your eyes, you realise that there has not been very much of it. Close the book.

34

The truckdriver explains that he would prefer you not to smoke and thanks you for your thoughtfulness in thinking to ask. In fact, he is so impressed by your conduct that he gives you a $20 note and tells you to spend it at the rodeo. He drops you at the entrance to the Owaka Domain. Go to 39.

35

You steal to the edge of the clearing. You see rough-looking men clad in black overalls and balaclavas. They do not look like the sort of people you are used to, but you step forward boldly.

Well, what a surprise! You have stumbled on a film crew who are making a television mini-series about a gang of takahe smugglers. The smugglers are foiled by a group of brave children. But everyone is extremely despondent. Apparently one of the young stars, a boy of about your own age, has had a terrible accident. His foot has been crushed in a gin trap. He had to be winched out by helicopter. The whole project may have to be abandoned.

One of the film crew has been staring at you in an odd way. He whispers something in the director's ear. 'Well', says the director, 'it's worth a try. He looks just right. You never know, it might be the answer to all our troubles.'

The director asks you if you would be willing to take the injured boy's place. He says that you are obviously talented; even more important, you look just right. You are thoughtful for a moment. It is sad that your big chance should depend on the misfortunes of another, but it would be foolish to turn down such an opportunity. You will probably become famous and wealthy. The series will be shown on Irish and Scandinavian television.

You say yes, you'll give it a go. All the members of the film crew cheer. If they had hats rather than balaclavas they would throw them in the air. So would you. What an ending this has turned out to be! And in career terms it is really much more like a beginning. Close the book.

36

You are in a dimly lit hotel bar. There is a smell of smoke and urine. At one end of the bar men are playing pool. From time to time they grind their cigarettes out on the carpet. A radio broadcasts commentaries from the night trots at Forbury.

In another part of the bar men are gathered around an old white-haired man. He looks poor but he is the centre of attention: everyone listens to him closely. You edge towards the group, trying to keep as inconspicuous as possible.

The old man is undoing his fly. He takes out his penis. All the men lean over and look at it. Then they each give him a $5 note. They joke and call him Fishhead.

'Yes,' says the old man. 'Maureen was never much struck on it, God rest her soul. But it was her I had it done for really. She was a Doolan when we got married, couldn't eat meat on Fridays.'

Rough male laughter fills the bar. You join in, but as you do so you feel a hand on your shoulder. You swing quickly around, ready to face this new challenge. Galloping Minerva! It is a policeman. You have been arrested for under-age drinking! Go to 37.

37

After a night in the cells, the friendly men on the duty watch at Dunedin Central Police Station give you a hearty breakfast and drop you on the road to Invercargill, just south of the Mosgiel turn-off. You shudder as they tell you what your fate will be should you show your face around these parts again.

You trudge south for several days, sleeping rough and begging for food at friendly farmhouses. On one occasion hunger drives you to eat a dead hedgehog. It is flat and full of maggots. Ugh!

Late one afternoon, not far from Milton, you see a big old man wearing a red-and-black-check Swanndri. He makes strange keening noises, and from time to time he seems to bend and peer into the roadside ditch. There is something familiar about the bent, stumbling figure. If you wish to approach him and strike up a conversation, go to 17. If you decide not to risk it, you can try and wave down a passing vehicle, in which case go to 25.

38

But flight is hopeless. Steel doors slide silently down, sealing off the openings at either end of the granite cavern. You swing around bewildered, knocking over several jars. Their ghastly contents spill across the rock floor. Herr Schneidermann has superhuman strength. He picks you up as if you are a feather; within minutes you are tied once again to the operating table.

'Now let me see,' says Herr Schneidermann. 'You are a foolish creature — without doubt a suitable candidate for brain enhancement. But you have destroyed many of my prize exhibits. You have severely reduced the range of choice…' He stares at you, and thoughtfully pops a black jelly bean into his mouth.

At last he picks up a jar and puts it down on a small table just behind your head. You strain and strain but cannot turn to read the label. Soon you feel yourself losing consciousness. You will wake again, but in what condition will you wake? And will you still be you? Go to 50.

39

Well, what an unexpected treat! You'll have the time of your life here! You ride a wild steer. You try a bucking bronco. You chase a slippery pig. Spectators laugh, but they are on your side, it is all good fun. You are given a free hotdog for being such a good sport.

You stroll around watching folks enjoy themselves. You win a frozen chicken on the chicken wheel. You watch the Owaka and District Highland Pipe Band. You also watch a team of marching girls, the Tapanui Pipettes. They tell you that they practise at least three evenings a week. They tell you about Tapanui's farm machinery museum. They tell you how they hope to go to the Edinburgh Tattoo one day, it is just a matter of doing all the fundraising. On a sudden impulse you give your chicken to the prettiest marching girl. 'Good luck to you, lassie,' you say.

Now a brightly coloured stall catches your eye. A sign says: 'How Many Jelly Beans in the Jar?' You see a glass jar filled to the brim with black jelly beans. Black ones are your favourite.

You decide to have a go. To your surprise, you guess the exact number: 1046! Go to 48.

40

You rub the Pounamu Decoder between your hands until it takes life from your warmth and begins to glow richly. At first you cannot make out what the mysterious alien is saying, but eventually the words come clear:

> delays in train, steamer, motor, air or other causes... not liable for injury, sickness, weather, strikes, war, quarantine, or other injury damage loss accident delay or irregularity however and by whomsoever cause and of whatever kind and subject to all such terms and conditions as set down in the brochure itinerary prospectus and entirely at customer risk and liability. Tour cost does not include baggage insurance, dry cleaning, afternoon teas or optional day trip to Franz Josef. Only upon written application will itemisation of costs be rendered.

You are puzzled by these comments, and come to the conclusion that direct mind implant of important information might be better after all. Go to 26.

41

The strange man introduces himself. He tells you that his name is Schneidermann. Wait! Haven't you heard this name before? The fact that he addresses you in a thick German accent and stands at attention as he does so leads you to wonder if he is not in fact the infamous Nazi brain surgeon, the one who was presumed dead at the end of World War II. The one who loved classical music.

Herr Schneidermann explains that you are in an artificial cavern deep below the glowworm caves at Lake Te Anau. An elaborate system of conduits and corridors connects it to the control centre of the hydro-electric power project at Manapouri's West Arm. Herr Schneidermann tells you that he has tapped into New Zealand's electricity supply: he will need a massive concentrated electrical charge at the point of Transplant Activation.

He wheels you over to the shelves on which are ranged the glass jars you had spotted earlier. Their hideous contents pulse slowly, like living things. Oh no! You begin to put two and two together! You strain your eyes, and at last you can read the labels. 'The Brain of Captain Cook.' 'The Brain of Te Rauparaha.' 'The Brain of Samuel Marsden.' There are row upon row of them. 'The Brain of Richard Seddon.' 'The Brain of Minnie Dean.' 'The Brain of Colin Meads.' Sitting by itself on the top shelf is a jar whose label reads: 'The Brain of Katherine Mansfield'. But this jar differs from its fellows. It seems to be full of black jelly beans.

'Now let me see,' says Herr Schneidermann, looking at you thoughtfully.

You stare into his cold, gloating eyes and realise that your situation is desperate. You have stumbled into the midst of some fiendish experiment. You must act, and quickly.

With one superhuman effort you strain at your bonds and burst free. If you have the Swiss Army Knife you should attack at once and rid the world of this madman once and for all. If so, go to 29.

If you think the better plan is to flee through the underground labyrinth, go to 38.

42

You rub the Pounamu Decoder until it glows with a deep, glacial fire. This is what you hear:

I think I was in love with you
But you know that feeling goes.
Still I'll try to get to like you
In your cowboy clothes.

The cheeky fantail repeats his song over and over. What can the strange words mean? Are they a warning? 'Goes' and 'clothes' makes for a rather feeble rhyme. Perhaps it would all sound better with acoustic guitar accompaniment?

But these are rather pointless speculations. You may as well try your luck with one of these passing cars. Go to 25.

43

You step through the Portal of the Past. It shimmers; you seem to float; all is darkness. Then the darkness lifts. You look about you. You are in a hotel bar. There is a smell of smoke and urine. In a corner men are playing darts. From time to time they swear and grind their cigarettes out on the lino floor. A voice on the radio is talking about the track at Wingatui.

Over by the bar, men are gathered round a red-haired man. You guess he is in his thirties. His hair is very short; he has ugly ears which stick out. But everyone is listening to him carefully. You edge towards the group of men.

What a strange sight! The red-haired man is undoing his fly. He takes out his penis. All the men lean over and look at it. There is something blue on it. Then they each give him a silver coin.

'Yes,' says the man, 'a good half crown's worth. I got that tattoo done in Singapore. I wasn't sure what kind of fish to get, but I knew the wife like groper.'

The men laugh. They joke and call him Fishhead. You join in the rough male laughter, though something makes you feel your visit here is drawing to a close. You sense inner molecular disturbance. What is happening? Are you being returned to the alien spacecraft? And are you going back to the present? Or is it your fate to be trapped here in the past, in the days before decimal currency?

You need not fear. You are travelling back to the present. But to discover what awaits you there, go to 21.

44

Time passes. You are delirious, beset by fitful dreams. But at last you regain consciousness. Through dark branches you glimpse a few pale stars. Imperceptibly, the dawn gains dominion; the first rays of the new day's sun come sifting through the soft canopy of green. Birds flit from branch to branch. Native pigeons, already heavy with berries, peer curiously at you. Inquisitive fantails dart above your head, always just out of reach; and soon the flute-like notes of the tui herald the glories of another day. Now the bellbird joins its singing to the music of its fellows: already you begin to feel restored, caught up in the rich, soothing harmonies of the rain forest.

But one bird swoops low, urging and urging its song at you, a cascade of sobbing notes. Is it trying to tell you something? Does it sound notes of welcome, or of woe?

If you have the Pounamu Decoder, go to 16.
If not, go to 45.

45

It is time to be on your way. You stare carefully around you. There are signs of a track leading south from the clearing. Perhaps you should go that way? Or you can follow the little creek downstream. That is something you are supposed to do if you are lost in the bush. Follow water downstream. Maybe you will eventually come to the Pacific coast.

If you decide to follow the track, go to 20.
If you think it wiser to follow along the bank of the creek, go to 30.

46

You wake, your eyes dazzled by bright lights. You are lying on your back, bound and unable to move. The place you are in is somehow like an operating theatre, except that it seems to be underground. The walls are composed of roughly hewn stone. Laser beams stab through the air. You see computers, control panels, retorts, and test-tubes.

On the far side of the room are shelves lined with jars. Each jar has a tube running into it, and each is filled with a curious grey sponge-like substance. There are labels on the jars, but they are too far away for you to read them.

You manage to turn your head and look in the other direction. An old man clad in a white gown sits watching you. He has cold, steel-blue eyes. As his eyes meet yours, a smile begins to flicker on his face, as if he has just seen the point of a joke, one which has been puzzling him for rather a long time.

'For pity's sake!' you cry. 'Who are you? *What* are you? What is this place?'

Go to 41.

47

Well done. You are wise and sensible. The white powder was cyanide poison, laid for possums. If you had tasted it, you would have died instantly. As it is, you will probably die very slowly, perhaps of hypothermia, for your situation is hopeless.

But you have shown splendid qualities of character, and you are to be reprieved. Know then that you have been granted a second chance to turn the pages of adventure. Return at once to the beginning and make a better choice at every point of change.

48

You go home, clutching your jar of jelly beans. It has been a wonderful day, you truly know the meaning of a phrase like 'tired and contented'. And what a story you have to tell! The cheeky escapades of Douglas the Elf... Those long summer days with Frederick and Karla... Miriam. Especially Miriam. That night by the Pomahaka River... White-water rafting on the Shotover... Croissants at Milford Sound... The Whitebait Museum at Okarito... Your mind is a whirl of competing memories. As your head sinks into the pillow and you start drifting off to sleep, you realise you are still clutching the Pounamu Decoder, the Jump Thermos or the Swiss Army Knife, whichever it happens to be. So it was all true! It really happened! Close the book.

49

A place of darkness. Mist and shafts of light. As in a dream you see a gigantic floating tongue appear before you. Perhaps it is a hologram, some kind of projection. You can see the tastebuds sticking out, pink like the undersides of mushrooms.

The tongue is making a series of sounds, not music but not words either. It starts to float towards you. You wonder if you should run but realise with a start that you are floating too. What should you do? The tongue has started licking you! Apparently that is what it wants to do.

Fool! you should have *swum* away. A tongue implies a mouth, and this tongue happens to be the visible part of an invisible mouth. You are being ingested by your own story, swallowed whole. This is a humiliating fate, but more common than you might imagine. Close the book.

50

You wake in your very own bed. You can hear your father snoring in the adjoining room. Your mother pushes the door open. Allbran and apricots, very welcome indeed. All night you have tossed and turned, beset by fitful dreams. Something about a helicopter? a mad scientist? You cannot remember.

You are a fairly ordinary New Zealander, except that you have a small moustache — unusual in a boy of twelve — and you speak with a slight German accent. You are learning the violin, are good at sports, and one day you plan to go into politics.

You kiss your mother goodbye and walk down the path. It's an overcast morning, but you pick up your step, cheered by the prospect of another day at school. What is this? An indistinct, shuffling figure hails you from the opposite footpath. Can it be? Is it? Yes. No. Yes, it is Wairarapa, older now, but without doubt the same good-natured soul who worked so hard as honorary caretaker for the Kaitangata Volunteer Fire Brigade. He is holding a leather-bound book. He looks as if he has been expecting you.

'I have been reading your story,' he says, 'and I must say I find it rather disappointing. I was wondering if there was any chance of getting my money back?'

The poor old man is mad. His life is nearly over, while yours is just beginning. You step around him, then give your mother a cheery wave and continue on your way. You do not look back, but feel sure that both she and Wairarapa go on waving long after you have vanished from sight.

Jenny's Bicycle

She had what people are given to describe as heavy, sensuous lips: a kind of fracture that opened across her face. There was a story that her lips were filled with little bones. Men who had kissed her declared that they had felt them scraping together, or beating slowly like birds' wings against their necks. When I met her in George Street, I was thinking of something else entirely.

'I am going to Europe,' she said. When I expressed some interest, she told me that her grandfather in Scotland had offered her the use of his bicycle, and that she meant to ride with some close friends through France and Spain, perhaps even through North Africa. She had stopped me in the street because she had heard that I owned a bicycle with three gears and she wanted to practice hill-climbing. It was the right thing to do, as we discovered, because I was unable to refuse her request.

Three or four times afterwards we met for coffee. On each occasion she was utterly exhausted. There was sand in her hair, which she combed out over the floor. She barely sipped her coffee. Once we went to a film, to sit in the dark. Her eyes hurt her. 'It's very good of you,' she said, 'to lend me the bicycle, considering we hardly know each other. I could never survive on the Spanish highways without this initial experience.' She told me about her Scottish grandfather, who owned a kilt and lived in Glasgow. He had promised to pay her fare to Europe. We talked right through the film, which was a horror story called *Psycho*. One day she rode all the way to Waikouaiti and back. It took six hours, because she had to push the bike up some of the hills.

'Still,' I said, 'it would be all right coming down.' While she was there, she had swum at the beach. I asked her if she had seen any sharks, and she said no.

In March 1966 a group of us were sitting drinking coffee. We had spread newspaper on the floor; we expected her to arrive at any moment. In the past at least two of us had kissed her, and we had a conversation about that. Then we considered the question of whether New Zealand's economic future lay in South East Asia. I remember that we all thought it probably did. As it turned out, we talked for nearly three hours, quite forgetting why we were there. Some of us made our way round to her room in Dundas Street. The door was wide open; pearls lay on the floor, and it was obvious to us all that they had been torn from a woman's neck. There were signs of a recent struggle. Without expecting such an event, we knew at once that we had come too late. I looked around for my bicycle, but it seemed to be gone, although I found the pump in the hall. It didn't matter. I had decided to do without it and intended to go to Australia to earn some money and buy a car.

How easy it is to confuse the event with the fact, I suppose. Certainly it was bones, if comparisons are to be made at all. Yet some took to a different story, attractive enough in its fashion, swearing black and blue that her lips were filled with tiny pearls, the kind that Japanese women dive for, naked, and deep into the water.

Nonchalance
or The New Land: A Picture Book

1. *The bishops*

The bishops come ashore. Tell me, they say, what is the name of this country? Does everyone here speak English or is it just the one or two of you? Please understand that we shall need hotel accommodation only until we have made somewhat more permanent arrangements. Be particularly careful with the blue suitcases, they contain flutes and ammunition. And here, sailing up the harbour, is the ship which brings the soldiers' wives.

2.

The wives come ashore. Here are the wives in the museum, their first real expedition from the hotel. What is this brown thing? asks one. Does it do something important? Can we take photographs in here or must we buy the postcards? In that case where is the *bureau de change*, the *cambio*, the *wechsel*?

And here is violent death, the brown thing. Here is sunset in the park, the first light of dawn, the flag flapping. The soldiers' wives are wondering about the harbour-lights tour. They have been told that the harbour-lights tour is excellent value for money, but they have only recently arrived and they want to sit down for a bit and think about it properly.

3. *Getting off to a good start*

The first step is to approach local inhabitants as if you are their guest. Move slowly. If possible, acquire a few words of local greeting and repeat them to everyone you meet. Hold out your hand to those you meet in a gesture that includes them in your experience. If you are male, be circumspect in your dealings with the local womenfolk. If you are female and alone, be glad that you are you, on the move and pleasing yourself most of the time.

4. *Making the characters come alive as individuals*

This can be done in a number of ways, but many new authors imagine it is all done by giving a description of clothing, whereas this doesn't really help. Picture a group of soldiers, all dressed in exactly similar clothing, and think of what makes each one an individual. How could you describe one of them in order to distinguish him from his fellows?

It can't be done by describing the clothing, so something else has to be considered. Well, one man might have, say, a ginger moustache, another may have huge hands, a third may walk as though expecting to fall down a flight of steps at the very next stride.

5. *The soldiers*

The soldiers are all at the front, from which word rarely gets back. Occasionally a private note to a loved one is intercepted and sold on the streets by enterprising youngsters. But most visitors are too embarrassed to purchase them; local residents do not usually have the money.

6.

Here is a photograph of the first flag, which was run up on the first sewing machine, which should be in the museum but has not survived. A soldier gazes up towards the flag, his face alight with expectation. And here is a photograph of the boat with its cargo of bishops looking disappointed (a) at the tiny jetty and (b) at the rather sparse welcoming party. Tell me, they say, what is the name of this country? Do you always have such beautiful weather?

7. *Giving and getting*

Not all of your contact with local people will involve getting something from them. Don't forget that you have a unique opportunity to bring them something from your own culture. Go ahead and show them what it looks like: try postcards, or magazines. If you have a camera, let the local people, especially the children, look through the viewfinder. Put on a telephoto so they can get a new look at their own countryside. Take along an instant print camera, photograph them and give them the ensuing print. Most important: *become involved.* Carry aspirins to cure headaches, real or imagined. If someone seems to need help, why not lend a hand? Contribute yourself as an expression of your culture.

8. *Another thing*

Another thing. On some of the more travelled routes the local children, used to being given sweets by passing soldiers, will swarm around, their sticky hands held out for more. The best course is to smile (always) and refuse them. Show them pictures, your favourite juggling act or a noble piece of stone (e.g. Edinburgh Castle). Then give them something creative, like pencils.

9. *The sadness competition*

The soldiers' wives are enjoying a night out. They have a block booking at the monthly sadness competition. Of course, they are only spectators, crammed into the back stalls, although as one of them (Irene) says to another (Trudy), sometimes the way you end up feeling, you might just as well be up there with the sailors as sitting down here watching. Trudy pulls a face, entering into the spirit of things.

The entrants are all sailors, far from home. The rules require contestants to think of something sad, so that the feeling will visibly transform their faces. As well, they must supply the saddest word they know and repeat it several times. The best words tend to be those like 'nonchalance', for they are filled with the sadness of seeming more sophisticated than the states of mind to which they refer. Many contestants concentrate their thoughts upon the ordinary sadness of the past — the oceans crossed, the lands and cities never to be regained, the families and sweethearts left behind, a single half-remembered cadence...tra la. Others prefer to think about the future, the emptiness of everything to come.

Tonight's winner is a young sailor. It turns out that he has been thinking of his present circumstances, which he defines in a word: 'unlimitless'. After his victory walk, he is bound hand and foot and taken away. He will go forward to the next round.

(All the same, said Trudy, I think I will just go on back to the hotel if that is all right with the rest of you. This has been quite enough excitement for me for one night! But aren't things getting off to a wonderful start!)

10. *A letter from the front*

My dear Irene,

What a snug little place this is! After a hard day of manoeuvres, a quiet smoke and a read in such comfortable surroundings are indeed something to look forward to. But how much more delightful this spot would be if it were your home as well as mine! Let us hope this dream will be fulfilled at no very distant date!

Could you have seen how eagerly I tore open your letter you would have felt well repaid for your trouble in writing it. What delightful things it contains, I can hardly bring myself to believe that it is I to whom all the sweet and tender things are said!

My darling, your sweet letter makes it very hard for me to curb my impatience until the day when we shall be together always. I wonder if you too sit and muse over our future home. Have you planned it just as you want it? Somehow I feel you have, and I, too, seem to know just what those plans are, for our tastes and ideas are so similar that were you to arrange every detail of our house, I'm sure I should not have a single alteration to suggest. Write again soon, my darling, for your letters charm away the pain and weariness of this ghastly war.

Your loving
'Ginger'

11. *First things first*

The first Highland Pipe Band. The first Amateur Weightlifting Association. The first affiliated branch of Alcoholics Anonymous. The first Shipwreck Relief Society. The first Mission to Seamen. The first Coopworth Sheep Society. The first Association of Teachers of Speech and Drama. The first one-armed bandit. The first alcoholic.

The first honeymoon hotel. The first Returned Services Association. The first accountant. The first tourist hotel with full en suite facilities. The first Santa Gertrudis Breeders Society. The first Association of Beauty Therapists. The first Australian Ambassador. The first Russian Ambassador. The first baby. The first newspaper, with a photograph of the first baby. The first Licensing Trust. The first New Zealand Ambassador. The first cuckoo.

12. *First things first (continued)*

The first school which the first baby will attend. The first Minister of Education. The first Volunteer Fire Brigade. The first American Ambassador. The first employed person. The first unemployed person. The first turning on the right. The first turning on the left. The first public lending library. The first massage parlour. The first overdue book. The first State lottery. The first free elections. The first death from natural causes. The first headstone. The first Esperanto meeting. The first campaign to lower the drinking age. The first film society. The first chamber music concert. The first street riots. The first Alfa Romeo Owners' Club. The second New Zealand Ambassador. The first Guild of Agricultural Journalists. The first dealer gallery. The first light of dawn.

13. *Dealing with deserters, individual prisoners, spies, negotiators, contingents of prisoners*

Take off your shoes. Empty your pockets. Cut the lining of your coat open. The lining of your hat. Have you any letters or other papers on you? Give me your memorandum book. What branches of the service? Are the troops well clothed, well cared for, and in good spirits? Are you here to negotiate? Who sent you? What do you want? Follow me. If you show yourselves willing and obedient, you have nothing to fear. Right (left) turn! March! Halt!

Are you hungry? Are you cold? Do you possess your own bishopric? Is it nearby? Can we journey there on foot? On the other side of the ranges? Beyond the seas? Please write your answer on this sheet of paper which I have brought with me expressly for the purpose. The ambulance will fetch you very soon. Remain quietly in a lying position. Sleep soundly. I will stay with you. Tomorrow we will make a start on expressions pertaining to conduct.

14. *The first short story*

'I was lying on the hillside in the sun, minding my own business as you might say, just soaking up the unfamiliar sunshine and wondering vaguely about the details of my life. My flute lay beside me. My shovel lay beside me. I was resting after my labours. Suddenly I was aware that men with guns were gathered round about me, one of their number crying loud above the chatter of the rest, "Are you the dying man?"'

15. *A letter from the front*

Dear Trudy,

It is useless for me to pretend that your letter was not a great blow, but at the same time I must confess that I had a feeling that your answer would be 'No'. At the moment I feel as though I shall not be able to stand it, for you are very, very dear to me, but I shall try to put the best complexion on the matter and bear my grief like a man.

It will, I think, be better for both of us if we do not see each other again for some little time, after which I hope we shall be able to meet again as really good friends. I would fight no longer in this ghastly war if I did not believe in some sort of future — for all of us. Your happiness means so much to me that, if I know you are happy, I am sure I shall, in time, come to look upon the world as a place not quite so lonesome and cold as it seems at this moment.

Always your sincere friend,
'Ginger'

16. *Plots to avoid*

(a) Plots with a sex motif.
(b) Where religion plays a dominating role.
(c) Plots where sadism or brutality appear.
(d) Plots with a basis of divorce.
(e) Plots where illness or disease must be emphasised.
(f) Plots dealing with harrowing experiences of children.
(g) Plots dealing with politics.
(h) Plots where a criminal succeeds in escaping justice.
(i) Plots that just don't go anywhere, e.g. 'The king died and then the queen went to the pictures.'

17. *Characters to avoid*

(a) Those with impediments of speech.
(b) Those with ugly physical infirmities.
(c) Idiots or those mentally afflicted.

There are exceptions to this of course, but for the beginner, the rule should be, avoid these types of people.

18. *Photographs*

The procession of coaches winds up the hill. Yo-ho-ho. The sailors are playing their flutes and drinking hard liquor, doing the things that come naturally to hard seafaring men. Each year, at this time, they make this expedition. They bring with them their photographs, captured images of bodies of water they have crossed: the Andaman Sea, the Tasman, the Yellow and Red Seas, the Ross Sea, the Sea of Okhotsk, the Java Sea.

Now they are digging holes in the green hillside, below the ancient fortifications. Custom requires one hole for every photograph. The coach drivers, bored, lean against their vehicles, rolling cigarettes. They have seen this sort of thing before. After the sailors have buried their photographs of water (the Andaman Sea, the Tasman, the Yellow and Red Seas, the Ross Sea, the Sea of Okhotsk, the Java Sea), they will eat their cut lunches, climb aboard the coaches and head on back to town.

19. *Don't forget to communicate*

This terrible lack of communication that arises many times in the work of new writers has already been dealt with to some extent. You, the author, conjure a vivid series of scenes in your mind and, satisfied yourself, fail to put down the transitional links that make the tale fully comprehensible to a stranger reading it.

You, the author, know that your female character has now left the museum and struck up a conversation with a young sailor who speaks one of the minor languages of sadness. But the reader cannot read your mind — the reader can only read what you have put on paper, which may not be enough.

And don't forget to foreshadow. If one of your characters is going to make use of a gun, then let the reader know well beforehand that a gun exists. Bang!

20. *Hope for the future*

But look at this, it is the first baby. The first newspaper, with a photograph of the first baby. This is good news to be able to carry on the first day after the dummy runs! The news from the front is sparse and is tucked away on the inside back page. The comics page is relatively unsophisticated. The correspondence column carries (1) a message from the bishops, expressing pleasure at the generous response to the first street appeal; (2) a letter about rising unemployment; (3) a request for pen-pals from Japan. There are only a few classified advertisements, but at least it is a start. The comics page is relatively unsophisticated. The whole thing probably needs a crossword or a few more photographs. A picture of one of those beauty spots where the trees come right down to the water: that would do.

21. *The black bird of my heart*

A sailor is singing. He has laid aside his flute and he sings in a voice that may or may not be carried out to sea. It depends on the wind, on the time of day, on the circumstances. He is young, the sailor, he is nonchalant, and the song he sings was popular in the fifties, before he was born. As he walks along, sauntering inland, he looks as though he expects to fall down a flight of steps at the very next stride. An older sailor taught him the song, warning him that some of the words might well be misremembered.

My tears have washed 'I love you' from... tra la.

But after all, it is only a song like any other. The form is fine but we will not guarantee the content. It deals with clouds and manacles, cameras and repressive legislation, martial law and inner torment. It deals with the world as we know it, at the point where it is only half imagined. Were we to ask the sailor, of course, he would disagree. He believes it is a song about his sweetheart, about whom he is not really thinking; while the children, who have begun to crowd around him holding out their sticky hands for sweets, believe it to be otherwise again: a song about the next new land, the one which is travelling by word of mouth from a place beyond the ranges, which is as yet beyond reproach, still at the stage of making up its mind.